D0201441

DURARARA!!

DRRR!!
SH ×2

RYOHGO
NARITA

ILLUSTRATION
BY
SUZUHITO
YASUDA

"That ethical wall sure is thick."

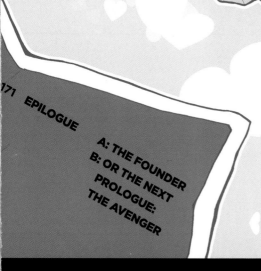

Akane Awakusu realized something.

The malice she once felt toward Shizuo Heiwajima had evolved into a kind of longing, but she knew it was something that could never be reciprocated.

She and Shizuo lived in different worlds in every possible sense.

She had no reason to defeat him anymore.

Or so she thought.

Nonetheless, she continued to push herself—as though seeking the limits of the human condition or what lay beyond even that.

All she wanted was to see what she admired from as close as possible.

She wanted to speak with Shizuo from the same level or as close as she could get.

She didn't feel a need for romance or anything of the sort.

171 EPILOGUE
A: THE FOUNDER
B: OR THE NEXT
PROLOGUE:
THE AVENGER

"All I could do was destroy the wall in front of me…"

She just wanted to see him.

When Shizuo understood there was someone who looked at him from the same level, what kind of smile would he wear?

Risking her entire life for that moment was worth it.

The path ahead seemed hard—impossible for a human, in fact.

She continued forward anyway, trusting that if she walked together alongside the man who once saved her life, she would surely, undeniably return the favor.

VOLUME 2

Ryohgo Narita
ILLUSTRATION BY Suzuhito Yasuda

NEW YORK

Durarara!! SH, Vol. 2
Ryohgo Narita

Translation by Stephen Paul
Yen On edition edited by Carly Smith & Yen Press Editorial
Cover art by Suzuhito Yasuda

This book is a work of fiction. Names, characters, places, and incidents are the product of the author's imagination or are used fictitiously. Any resemblance to actual events, locales, or persons, living or dead, is coincidental.

DURARARA!! SH Vol. 2
©RYOHGO NARITA 2014
Edited by Dengeki Bunko
First published in Japan in 2014 by KADOKAWA CORPORATION, Tokyo.
English translation rights arranged with KADOKAWA CORPORATION, Tokyo, through TUTTLE-MORI AGENCY, INC., Tokyo.

English translation © 2021 by Yen Press, LLC

Yen Press, LLC supports the right to free expression and the value of copyright. The purpose of copyright is to encourage writers and artists to produce the creative works that enrich our culture.

The scanning, uploading, and distribution of this book without permission is a theft of the author's intellectual property. If you would like permission to use material from the book (other than for review purposes), please contact the publisher. Thank you for your support of the author's rights.

Yen On
150 West 30th Street, 19th Floor
New York, NY 10001

Visit us at yenpress.com
facebook.com/yenpress
twitter.com/yenpress
yenpress.tumblr.com
instagram.com/yenpress

First Yen On Edition: August 2021

Yen On is an imprint of Yen Press, LLC.
The Yen On name and logo are trademarks of Yen Press, LLC.

The publisher is not responsible for websites (or their content) that are not owned by the publisher.

Library of Congress Cataloging-in-Publication Data
Names: Narita, Ryōgo, 1980– author. | Yasuda, Suzuhito, illustrator. | Paul, Stephen (Translator), translator.
Title: Durarara!! SH / Ryohgo Narita ; illustration by Suzuhito Yasuda ; translation by Stephen Paul.
Other titles: Durarara!! (Light novel). English
Description: First Yen On edition. | New York : Yen On, 2021.
Identifiers: LCCN 2021009783 | ISBN 9781975322779
(v. 1 ; trade paperback) | ISBN 9781975323462 (v. 2 ; trade paperback)
Subjects: CYAC: Fantasy. | Tokyo (Japan)—Fiction.
Classification: LCC PZ7.1.N37 Dur 2021 | DDC [Fic]—dc23
LC record available at https://lccn.loc.gov/2021009783

ISBNs: 978-1-9753-2346-2 (paperback)
978-1-9753-2347-9 (ebook)

1 3 5 7 9 10 8 6 4 2

LSC-C

Printed in the United States of America

CONJOINING CHAPTER

CONJOINING CHAPTER
The Commentator: Or Perhaps an Informant's Monologue

Shinjuku—several years ago

Hi, how have you been?

If I'm being honest, I don't actually care. Maybe you've been on top of the world, or maybe you've been frozen with despair and ennui. It doesn't matter to me.

But what do you want with me?

Getting involved with this ne'er-do-well will only lead to misfortune. I'm sure you're old enough to understand that by now, right?

Oh, it's about the Headless Rider again?

We talked about what to do if you encounter the Headless Rider in person before…in Ikebukuro, as I recall.

I mentioned that people react in a variety of ways when faced with the abnormal—whether monster or alien or even a fellow human being.

When it comes to other humans, the results will differ depending on whether the subject is a person you're meeting in the flesh or a person who's only been a vague, shadowy rumor.

Human imagination is stimulated the most when it attempts to grasp something that is unknown and unidentified but which undeniably exists.

If you've shared a conversation with the Headless Rider, then there's nothing vague about its existence. You might not know *what* it is, but you know *that* it is. You'd know it's an intelligent being capable of conversation.

That's all it takes to eliminate that vagueness, but you'll never get that far if you haven't met the person.

If someone said, *The Headless Rider's pretty cool and understands Japanese fluently*, the hypothetical listener who has never seen this figure would only take that statement at face value if they truly trusted the speaker.

This is where we reach a kind of branching point.

Obviously, the Headless Rider is an anomaly in our society, right?

It's obvious from the writhing shadows and horse-turned-silent-motorbike that present-day science cannot understand it.

Many people think it's all just a fancy trick, while others think, *This means the entire world will change…*

Perhaps half of them are afraid and half of them are excited.

Meanwhile, all the atheists and skeptics of the paranormal are shitting their pants over it.

Actually, I shouldn't lump them together; I've seen atheists who think paranormal phenomena could be real, and I've seen devout religious folks who deny any possible existence of the paranormal.

But setting that aside…that's where you'll find a world that surpasses human understanding.

People respond to such a world in various ways.

For example, one emotion might be…admiration.

Were you expecting me to say *fear*?

That might be the ordinary answer. However, some people admire the inexplicable and find excitement in what science cannot explain. They're real, and they're out there.

Furthermore, these individuals feel society has trapped them on all sides; they're stuck in a situation they cannot deny or escape. They might wish for the entire world to be a lie—that the real world is a much better place for them.

But nothing changes, does it?

They have neither the power nor the will to escape on their own.

So instead, they yearn.

For what?

A chance!

It doesn't matter how trifling it might be—*they want a chance to turn the world upside down!*

Haven't you ever used your imagination?

What if I had special powers?

What if I could run faster?

What if I was stronger?

What if I was smarter?

What if I was more attractive?

What if I could sing better?

What if I could draw better?

What if I could understand how other people feel?

What if I had psychic abilities?

It starts off as the most insignificant desires.

A yearning for a version of yourself in possession of *something else.*

However, that eventually morphs into hatred of reality. The discontent at your own powerlessness builds as you find you are unable to escape yourself.

We're not talking about comic book powers like shooting flames from your hands. It could be something as mundane as a bullied child finding the little courage it takes to confide in someone, or an abused child at home finding the tiny malice needed to give their parent a little push from the top of the stairs, or even the meager literary ability to write a diary of fantasies about all the ways your hated enemy could die.

But if I'm being honest, it doesn't have to stem from such dark emotions—some people out there get so tired of how boring everyday life is.

All those various frustrations with reality eventually converge on the same wish: *If I can't change, then the world should change instead.*

What would you do if the thing that might bring change to the world suddenly showed up on the TV screen? Something capable of breaking through the laws of physics and the common sense of society. Something capable of changing the very structure of the world.

Just think about it.

Let's say the Headless Rider is a ghost, and that fact could be proved. That would prove the existence of an afterlife.

And once that's understood, it would completely change the world.

I wonder if there would be fewer people committing suicide or *more*?

If you knew life after death was absolutely guaranteed, would you kill yourself, feeling secure in that knowledge? Or would you despair at the thought of your consciousness continuing after death and decide against it?

Of course, it's not exactly fair to use such childish examples, but human beings allow their lives to be dictated by very foolish things.

Maybe the people who see the greatest importance in the Headless Rider are not those who have met the rider in person but the ones who are watching from a slight distance instead.

To a certain kind of person, the Headless Rider represents hope.

Everyone has to deal with certain undeniable realities. Ultimately, it comes down to how each person chooses to react.

Some people will reject certain realities and refuse to accept them, while others might give up and go along with the very same realities. Some might even embrace them, of course.

Everyone deals with a reality they cannot escape, to some extent.

So no matter what path you choose, each one represents the contours of a human life. I wouldn't deny you that choice—even if the rest of the world would call it a terrible mistake.

Because, you see, I love human beings.

♂♀

Present day—morning, Tatsugami household

"Himeka, you're doing all right, aren't you?" asked Himeka Tatsugami's mother in a tremulous voice. She looked slightly older than her years, and her face was worn-out. "You aren't going to disappear on us, are you?"

Himeka had an older and younger sister, both missing. The two of them had said, *"I might be able to meet the Headless Rider,"* shortly before they vanished.

Half a month had passed since anyone had last seen them. The family submitted missing persons reports to the police, who had made no progress on finding them.

With two of her daughters going missing at once, there was no wonder Himeka's mother looked worn-out.

But Himeka knew that her mother was suffering long before this happened.

And even if both sisters were safe and sound, nothing about her mother's health would change.

The woman wasn't just tired. She was broken. Himeka would never say so aloud, but she had always known.

"Please, Himeka, I'm begging you. Don't leave me on my own. Especially not with *him*."

Himeka was well aware, of course, that "him" referred to her father.

And she was very familiar with the way the statement was delivered—not to Himeka's face but toward the wall of the hallway, forehead pressed against its surface, muttered through clenched teeth. This behavior had persisted for several years.

Her mother didn't speak with her forehead grinding against the wall all the time. It was more like a kind of spasm that happened about once a day.

The frequency hadn't increased after her daughters went missing, either. If anything, the utter, unaffected consistency made Himeka sad to think about.

But as sad as it was, Himeka's expression did not distort with grief. She was as cold and flat as ever while she stroked her mother's back. "It's all right, Mom. They'll be back very soon."

Either in response to Himeka or entirely by a coincidence of timing, her mother muttered, "It's the Headless Rider's fault."

"..."

Himeka said nothing as her mother mumbled and muttered under her breath to no one in particular.

"That thing took Aya and Ai... It's taking everything from me! Aaaaaah!" she screamed, her voice rising hysterically.

Himeka wrapped her arms around her mother's torso. "It's all right. It'll be all right, Mom."

These words washed over her mother like nothing. She continued hurling her words against the wall. "I knew it... I knew I should have *killed them* to stop them from going... I should have done whatever it took..."

"Mom..."

"It's true... I asked about it on the Internet...and everyone said such horrible things to me. Such incomprehensible things. I'm sure it was all the Headless Rider's doing. You understand, Himeka."

Despite being barely aware of her presence, Himeka's mother repeated her name throughout the screed. Himeka looked on her with neither anger nor mourning.

This was daily life to her—something she simply had to accept.

Although *acceptance* in this case was more like *resignation*.

And in the midst of the life she'd resigned herself to, she came into contact with something alien in her environment.

Not alien in the usual way, like the Headless Rider was.

Alien like a monster who took the form of a harmless-looking boy: Yahiro Mizuchi.

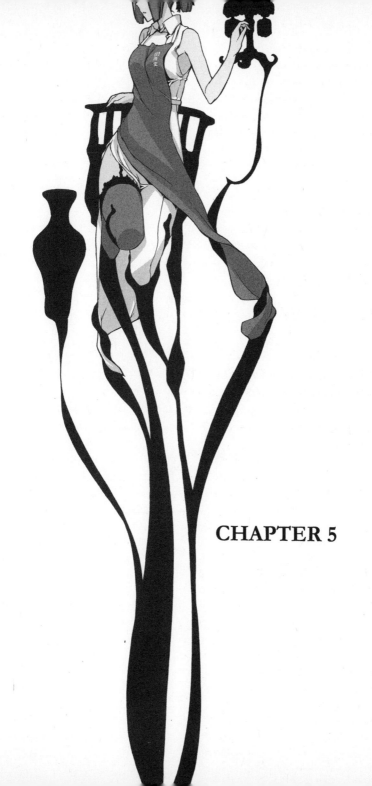

CHAPTER 5

CHAPTER 5 A
The Envoy

Ikebukuro—outside of Sonohara-dou Secondhand Shop

The store on the outskirts of Ikebukuro didn't quite blend in with its surroundings.

Situated in the middle of an ordinary residential neighborhood, a good walk from the shopping district near the station, was an old building combining a business storefront and the home attached to it.

Considering that it was a secondhand store, the run-down look actually suited its wares. Its exterior display window was cut directly out of the wall, offering a look at oddities such as a teacup with strange reddish-black coloring, paper currency that looked like nothing you'd ever seen before, and so on.

The door to the shop burst open, and a few young people emerged, wearing modern school uniforms.

"I'm glad I found a good radio," said a shy boy—Yahiro Mizuchi—clutching his new purchase to his chest. "Tatsugami, thanks for recommending this place to me."

The girl he was speaking to—Himeka Tatsugami—just shook her head. "Don't mention it. The shop happened to be nearby."

"Well, I got it for really cheap. That was a great bargain," Yahiro said, gazing at his not-so-new radio.

The frame was made of wood pieces fitted together, and there was a carved insignia of a rising dragon on the backside. The radio's dark mahogany finish made it look like it ran off a spring apparatus rather than batteries.

Despite the extremely rare and unique look of the radio, the woman running the shop gave him a stunning discount when she saw the Raira Academy uniforms.

"When I heard a graduate of Raira had just started this business, I thought it would be newer. I never imagined it'd look like it's been around for a century! And the girl running it was pretty hot, even with the glasses and boring clothes. You think she's got a boyfriend?" wondered a green-haired boy who had no interest in radios and little in common with the vibe of the shop—Kuon Kotonami. He thought back on the young store proprietor and continued to speculate inappropriately. "So does a girl that young really run the whole business on her own? That's wild, right? Doesn't she have a family?"

"Hmm…I'm not sure," Himeka said. "Some people helped with renovating when the business opened, I know."

"Are there lots of stores like this?" asked Yahiro, looking back over his shoulder at the receding building.

Himeka thought it over and replied, "Yes, I suppose there are a fair number of individually owned businesses. The general vibe is different depending on which station you're near, and there are lots of fascinating places to visit, so I'd recommend traveling around."

"Ohhh. Wow, Tokyo sure is incredible."

"You know this isn't just a Tokyo thing, right?" Kuon pointed out.

Yahiro shook his head. "Oh. Sorry. I've basically never been out of my hometown."

"Oh yeah? I'm surprised you decided to come to Tokyo, then. That's kinda weird," Kuon murmured distractedly, his attention drawn to Yahiro's radio. "So wait, you don't even have a TV in your place, and you're gonna let a radio be your only source of information?"

"I'm sure I'll be fine. I have a smartphone anyway."

"You'd rather have a phone than a TV? Kids these days. What social media are you on?"

"Social media?" Yahiro repeated, confused.

Stunned, Kuon could only shake his head. "Y'know, online social networks?" he explained. "Basically, any major app you use to communicate with a bunch of other people at once. You know, like Twittia, or Facemagazine, or Nixi, or FINE."

None of these rang a bell for Yahiro, however. Finally, he guessed, "Like chat rooms?"

"Oh…my god. I can't believe I'm hearing the words *chat room* in this day and age. That's amazing. Whatever. If you've got a phone already, I'll show you some good, free sites after this…"

Kuon was going to continue, but the tap of a car horn behind him broke his concentration.

"Huh?"

The trio turned around and saw a van coming to a stop. The passenger-side window rolled down, and a boy stuck his head out.

He was wearing another Raira Academy uniform and, at first glance, was the same age as the trio walking on foot. But he was older, in fact.

"…Kuronuma."

"There you are. Good thing your hair's so easy to spot."

"What's up? You told me you were too busy today to hang out, right?" Kuon said jovially to his friend. Yahiro and Himeka shared a quick glance.

At first glance, Kuronuma seemed like a perfectly nice boy, but the menacing look on the man driving and the black tint on all the rear windows spoke to a more threatening possibility.

Yahiro was confused—uncertain of how he should take this development—and received the full attention of their upperclassman in the passenger seat.

"Hey, Kuon…who are those kids?" he asked. But despite the plural, he was looking entirely at Yahiro, who assumed he was simply noticing the cuts and bruises on his face.

"Oh, they're from my class," said Kuon breezily. "That's Mizuchi, and that's Tatsugami."

"Ahhh. Well, I'm Aoba Kuronuma, third year. Nice to meet you."

"Hi…I'm Yahiro Mizuchi." He bowed. Himeka joined him and murmured a soft hello.

"Mizuchi, you said? You look hurt—are you all right?" Aoba asked, indicating the bruises on Yahiro's face.

"Yeah, I just fell down the stairs..."

"The stairs? Where?"

"Ummm...," Yahiro stammered, coming up short. He wasn't expecting to get a follow-up question to that explanation.

Kuon quickly butted in to rescue his friend. "Oh, at the station! The station! He came to Tokyo from a little place all the way up in the mountains, and he's not used to Tokyo crowds. He started feeling sick and just fell right down the stairs. I couldn't believe it!"

"Er, uh, yeah," Yahiro agreed, sanctioning Kuon's extremely smooth lies.

"Oh? Where'd you come from?"

"A hot springs town in Akita... Um, if you go east from Hachirogata, it's a village called Haburagi."

"Haburagi," Aoba repeated, committing it to memory, then beamed and said to Kuon, "So you're showing your friend around today, then."

"Yeah, basically."

"That's interesting. I didn't realize you were so helpful to other people." Then he turned to Yahiro and Himeka. "You should be careful. If you hang out with him, it'll lower your grades."

"Wha—? Aw, that's messed up, man... I might have green hair, but I'm actually a pretty good tutor," Kuon protested.

Aoba chuckled, ignoring his younger friend, and raised a hand. "Well, see you later. If you want to know about anything, feel free to ask me if you see me at school," he said, rolling up the passenger window and playing the role of the cool older guy.

The trio watched the van drive around the corner of a side street. It was Kuon who broke the ensuing silence with a deep breath and a laugh.

"Phew! Yikes, that was close. I can't believe the things he'll say, true or false. Don't worry too much about him, all right? I'm serious. For my sake, too."

"Well, I wasn't upset. He only made fun of you, not me," said Yahiro.

"And it's not like he said anything that was worth worrying about," noted Himeka.

Kuon shrugged uncomfortably. "Anyway, my point is, keep your distance around him."

♂♀

Inside the van

"You think that was getting too close?"

The van rolled away from the younger schoolmates.

The driver chewed noisily, smacking his gum, and continued, "Also, is that really the guy who went one-on-one with Shizuo?"

"Probably. Kuon gets around with lots of people aside from us, so the possibility is quite high," Aoba replied, looking bored. "I would have preferred to talk to him more, though."

"That's really him? The kid who fought Shizuo Heiwajima?" said Aoba's friend Yoshikiri from the back seat.

"I'm not certain, but I intend to find out."

"Yeah, but he just didn't seem like a fighter to me. Too quiet, right?"

Yoshikiri enjoyed fighting, so he had a knack for identifying people who possessed that same air of danger. He did not get that sense from Yahiro Mizuchi, whoever he was.

But Aoba thought over what he'd seen and asked Yoshikiri, "Did you see his hands?"

"Huh? Nah. Can't see 'em through the window."

"They were covered in scars."

To Aoba's eyes, Yahiro's hands were covered in aged scars, practically *painted* in them.

The boy couldn't have ended up with hands like those from normal circumstances, but Aoba chose not to bring it up on their first meeting.

Another guy in the back seat laughed and teased, "Oh yeah, like what? Did he have a scar from getting stabbed by a pen?"

"Shut up," snapped Aoba, his brows furrowed. He looked up at the ceiling of the car and murmured, "Kuon's probably up to something, I'm sure. And I'd like to have a way to contact him on my own, just in case. But I couldn't ask right then and there. That would've been weird."

Instead, he pulled out his phone and began an Internet search.

"Haburagi...Haburagi... Ahhh, here we go. Haburagi Village. That must be it."

The list of results had the home page of a hot springs inn on top, followed by tourism companies and personal blogs promising one of the "most overlooked spots in Japan for natural hot springs."

It took quite a while before he spotted the page for the village office, which told him that there wasn't much to Haburagi aside from its hot springs.

After that, he tried searching a few other keywords and made his way through user groups on various social networks, plus message boards for locals. A few minutes later, Aoba's eyes narrowed.

"Bingo."

He had found the message board of a town adjacent to Haburagi. In a thread for high schoolers to trade information, a post from about a week ago had some interesting information.

"The monster from Haburagi's going to high school in Tokyo."

"You mean Mizuchi?"

"Seriously?"

"I'm so glad. If he went to a public school, he'd be in ours."

"Yeah, the older guys were freaked out about it."

"This is great. Now I can actually enjoy high school!"

It was a very brief, informal kind of conversation, more like a chat room than a proper message board. But it was evidence enough for Aoba to feel confident about Yahiro's identity.

Inwardly smirking at the proof of his suspicions, he didn't let the smugness show on the outside. "Well, now the question is, what do we do? I'm curious about what Kuon thinks he's getting up to."

"What? If that kid thinks he can mess around behind our backs, we'll just kick his ass and that's that," snarled Yoshikiri menacingly.

"Not so fast," warned Aoba. "Don't strangle the goose that lays the golden eggs." His tone turned contemplative. "I suppose we could also wait and see how the others react. For one thing, I don't know what this promising young warrior is after in the first place."

The conversation inside the car dried up there and returned to the topic of their ordinary lives—at least, ordinary by their standards.

It was Aoba's blaring ringtone that seemed determined not to let them lapse back into comfortable topics.

"Hmm, I wonder who this is," said Aoba, glancing at the name on the phone display before he pressed the button to accept the call. He was briefly startled, then smirked to himself.

"Hello...? Yes, it's been a while. Right...I'm fine. Good, good... Oh please, don't sound so angry," he said, quite happily. The other Blue Squares in the car with him shared glances. He sounded polite, meaning that it was someone in a superior position, but more than that, they hadn't heard Aoba sound so delighted in ages.

A few of them assumed it was a call from Mikado Ryuugamine, but that idea quickly went out the window. Mikado had almost entirely cut himself off from people like them. At best, Aoba got to chat with him about harmless topics at school every now and then.

While they were busy guessing, Aoba smirked and leered. "Yes, if it's the one I'm thinking of, I can send you a headshot in a second."

But a second after that, a tiny amount of shock appeared in the midst of his smile.

Then he repeated the name, making sure he'd heard the other person right.

"You want...Himeka Tatsugami?"

♂♀

Raira Academy—a few days later

Raira Academy was already into a normal school schedule by now. Yahiro found that he not only was taking part in classes but also was not being shunned by everyone.

The bruises on his face had faded quite a bit, and he had removed his bandages. He looked almost back to normal. Himeka and Kuon were shocked at the speed of his recovery, but Yahiro had been dealing with sneak attacks and the like since he was a tiny kid; injuries were a familiar occurrence to him. If anything, he seemed more weirded out by *their* reaction.

His other classmates were alarmed by the bruises at first, but they warmed up to interacting with him as the marks healed. Still, with the prickly-looking Kuon hanging around all the time, very few of them talked with him more than absolutely necessary.

With the Shizuo Heiwajima fight in the past, Yahiro was grateful for a nice, quiet start to his high school career—but on this day, that tranquility came crumbling down at lunch.

Just a few minutes into the lunch period, Yahiro was wondering where he should eat the boxed lunch he brought from home when a girl's voice at the classroom door caught his attention.

"Miii-zuuu-chiii! Come out and plaaay!"

The other students still in the room looked up at the doorway, then back and forth between the girl standing there and Yahiro.

"Ah…ummm…Miss Orihara?"

"Bingo! Good job! You remembered me!" exclaimed the senior, sporting glasses and braids. She strolled right into the first-year classroom without any delay and plopped herself down right into Yahiro's chair. "Anyway, you got some time after school today?"

"Ummm, I'm on after-school duty for the library committee…"

"Oh! Then I'll go to the library to see you! There's lots I want to tell you!" Mairu said, despite having never been in a solo conversation with Yahiro before.

"Um, that makes it sound like you're just showing up to interfere with my job…"

"Hey, don't sweat it. I'll apologize to the library chairman for you. By the way, where's Kuon?"

"Probably up on the roof, I'd guess."

"Gotcha. Wonder if he's eating with Aobacchi and his friends."

Kuon was off doing whatever that was about, and Himeka had gone to the student store to buy lunch. Nobody else in the classroom was likely to bail Yahiro out of this situation—they just glanced at him from a distance across the room.

"I mean, if you want to talk, we can do it now…"

"Nope, not now. This isn't something to rush," she scolded and stuck her index finger vertically to her lips in a shushing motion. Then she held out the same finger and mashed it against his lips the same way.

"…?!"

"Don't worry, don't worry. Let's just wait until after school and talk about *allll kinds* of things we can't discuss here, m'kay?"

It was hard to tell if her grin was mischievous or sultry. In either case, she was soon out the door and out of his hair.

"Mizuchi, do you know her?" asked a few of the girls in class once Mairu was gone.

"I met her briefly a little while ago. What's she like?" he asked suspiciously.

The girls shared a look before answering, "Um…exactly the way she seems."

"She's pretty well known around school."

"Her twin sister is the vice president of the student council…"

"Just be careful of the Orihara sisters. Their fans are like cultists—both boys *and* girls—so watch out!"

It was a lot of information for Yahiro to take in at once, but none of it was very specific, and he came away feeling like he didn't understand her any better at the end of it.

The experience at the dojo and the conversation just now were enough to make clear what a chaotic personality she had. But what did a third-year girl want with him? Yahiro pondered this as he chatted with his classmates and prepared to eat lunch.

It's probably nothing that serious. Like something about the Headless Rider or maybe an invitation to join her dojo.

He imagined it would be something harmless and not worth worrying about. He could not have been more wrong.

Library—after school

"So hey! How did you fight on even footing with Shizuo?!" she asked, eyes sparkling.

Yahiro couldn't help but lean backward, his cheek twitching. "Wh-what do you mean?"

"C'mon, don't play dumb. We know the story already!"

"…Pure…respond…" [Just answer honestly.]

The way his eyes were wandering was anything but convincing—because two older girls were staring right at him from either side.

It wasn't just Mairu. Her big sister, Kururi Orihara, was with her, and they had cornered Yahiro in the library so they could pelt him with questions.

At the very least, they had a modicum of consideration for him and had avoided the busy hour at the library. Instead, they waited until nearly closing time, when virtually everyone had already left campus, before pouncing on Yahiro.

Meaning that he was attracting intense interest from two girls in the library after school, without anyone else around. Some people might find that to be a very appealing situation, but Yahiro was in anything but that kind of mood at the moment.

"Um, I honestly don't know what you mean…"

"Look, people got all kinds of pics of you in the act. It was from a distance so your face was hard to make out, but when the boy next to you has green hair—well, that makes it clear, doesn't it?"

"There are lots of people in Tokyo with green hair, aren't there?"

"…Here…mistake…?" [Are you sure you have the right idea about Tokyo?]

Yahiro was a poor liar, so the best he could do was try to avoid the eyes of the twin sisters. He was in a panic because he didn't think that anyone knew he'd been in a fight.

But he had sorely underestimated the information network of Ikebukuro.

Naturally, getting into a huge fight in the middle of the city was a big problem. But dealing with police was nothing unfamiliar to Yahiro.

No, the real problem was that this wasn't his home. His family wasn't here, and anything he did would come back on the Togusas, who were offering him a place to live. So in that sense, despite the lack of help from police, Yahiro was actually relieved they didn't show up the other day.

Losing to Shizuo Heiwajima helped blow off some of the steam, but deep down, he was ashamed of the hardwired nature that led him to get into so many fights, and more importantly, he was afraid the altercation would lead to him getting kicked out of school and sent back home.

To Yahiro, this city was the one place where he could feel actual hope about his new self.

He was grateful to his hometown. It offered security. But the hope that existed there was of peace and stability. If he stayed, he'd only be treated like a monster, and that negativity meant he would have to abandon any hope of change for the better.

But in a new place, there was possibility.

There was the Headless Rider, a true monster.

There was Shizuo Heiwajima, whom he fought with all his strength and still couldn't beat.

And there were friends who would accept him.

Yahiro was intoxicated with the dizzying pace of changes to his life.

But given his timid personality, it also terrified him.

Now that he finally had a new life, what about the possibility that it could all turn back into nothing?

"I…um…"

"It's fine—you don't need to hide it. We're not going to blame you for fighting or tell anyone about whatever you say."

"R-really?"

"…That…admit…" [Well, that counts as admission.]

"Oh!" he gasped, shocked at his lack of caution.

When he was back in Akita, his timidity made him extra careful, and he would never have answered that way. The realization stunned him; the culture shock of being in Tokyo had really softened up his mind.

Although in truth, it wasn't really Tokyo, just the lingering high of his fight with Shizuo Heiwajima.

Yahiro closed his eyes for a moment, then exhaled with resignation and admitted, "Yes…it's true. I had a fight with Shizuo Heiwajima…"

"I knew it!"

"…Surprise…" [That's amazing!]

"What?" he stammered, unable to fathom why the girls would be so excited about this. Every time people found out he'd been in a fight, they looked at him with fear and naturally drifted away.

That was how it always went.

But the reaction of these girls was impossible for him to gauge, based on prior experience.

Mairu said, "Well, I mean, it's incredible! You actually had a direct fight with Shizuo and held your own! It's like there's a brand-new hero in Ikebukuro or something, ya know?"

"Hero?"

"Yes, exactly. This place is always starving for the next story to talk about. If you announce your presence, you could be the entire talk of the streets!"

"I don't really have any intention of doing that," Yahiro said, his face darkening despite Mairu's praise.

I don't like being treated like I'm special, whichever way it happens to be. Besides, people called me a monster. It's beyond silly that I'd suddenly be a hero next.

"You don't? Well, that's a valid choice, too. I respect that," Mairu said.

"Thank you."

"But I think it's too late for that."

"Huh?" He raised his face.

Mairu explained, "You've already had a vivid Ikebukuro debut! You can try to lie low and hide, but the city isn't going to give you peace."

Ikebukuro—outside of Tokyu Hands

"Yo, Yahiro. Took you long enough."

They were at a huge intersection on the far side of Sunshine Sixtieth Floor Street, from the perspective of the train station. Nearby was the entrance to the Tokyu Hands department store, where the foot traffic was constant, day or night. It was a popular meeting spot because of its central location and easy access by subway along the way to the Sunshine City complex.

The trio decided to meet at six thirty and talk about what to do next.

"Sorry, I got caught in the library."

"Ugh. Was it Kuronuma?"

"No, the Oriharas."

"Oh, man, that's just as bad!" Kuon exclaimed and made a *rest in peace* praying gesture. Then he straightened up and asked, "So what did they want to talk about? I know they're all hot and bothered about some idol, so I assume they didn't confess their undying love to you."

"Yeah, we were just chatting," said Yahiro breezily, glancing briefly at Himeka.

There was no reason to let her know about what happened with Shizuo, he decided. Kuon seemed to pick up on that and didn't press the topic any further.

"Well, our school's got a lot of problem students, past and present."

"Oh, really?" Yahiro asked.

Himeka explained, "It was apparently rather famous for having lots of delinquents up until about a decade ago. It was called Raijin High School back then, but people say the school changed a lot when it became Raira Academy."

"Ohhh…"

"Anyway, let's get walking. I'll just show Yahiro around the town a bit, so we can go for a stroll, then get something to eat later and hash out our plans. Sound good?" Kuon chuckled, patting their shoulders.

The pair didn't really have a reason to refuse, so they let him push them along.

At this time, they didn't yet realize that a shadow was watching them with clear intent.

More than one, in fact.

♂♀

Ikebukuro—thirty minutes later

"There aren't as many people around here, are there?"

The trio was on a street a bit farther away from the shopping center. Since they'd just gone through a big tourist spot, Yahiro was a bit surprised at the change.

"Well, yeah," Kuon said. "Ikebukuro's hardly the only place in the world where a different parallel street might as well be a different city entirely. And it changes completely based on the time of day, too."

"Ohhh."

Up until middle school, Yahiro's village had been his entire world.

Because he knew every street like the back of his hand, the entire place was just *my village* in his mind, but now that he was in a new environment, even the smallest differences were novel and exciting.

His mind was occupied with thoughts of how the crowd density could be so different across such a small space—

—when an odd sensation caused him to stop in his tracks.

"What's the matter?" asked Himeka.

He didn't look at her. He was staring at the end of the street they were walking down.

"There's…something."

"Huh? Like what?" Kuon demanded, squinting.

It was just a normal alley, no different from any other. But…

"…Huh?"

In the darkness between streetlight and streetlight, there was shadowy space where it was truly empty, with no storefronts of any kind.

And within that darkness was an even deeper dark that stood out in relief.

"What *is* that…?" Yahiro wondered, squinting even harder. He noticed that something was floating within the gloom.

It was a yellow full helmet.

And thanks to online video sites, it was something that Yahiro recognized.

"…!"

His heart lurched.

The mass of darker shadow was coming closer to them, bit by bit. The thing took in the light of the overhead lamps, but did not reflect it. That just made the darkness stand out more clearly against its surroundings.

It was a shape anyone could recognize: a motorcycle.

Sitting atop a motorcycle without a headlight or license plate, dressed in a pitch-black riding suit, was *something else*.

The only extra detail of the shadow-shrouded thing was the helmet. In the darkness, it would have looked like a severed head floating in empty space.

There was no need to wonder about who this was.

Kuon recognized it, and gasped, "No way…"

Next to Yahiro, Himeka squeezed sweaty hands and said aloud what they all knew.

"The Headless…Rider…"

Her eyes were wide, and he could tell that her breathing had quickened. She watched with bated breath, and Yahiro worked through his clattering nerves to ask, "Um…are you all right?"

The note of quavering in his voice told him that he was quite agitated, too.

But though Yahiro and Himeka wore similar expressions, there was one fundamental difference between them.

Behind Yahiro's shock was elation and hope.

And behind Himeka's eyes was crystallized hatred and fear.

The reason he came to Tokyo was right here in front of him.

The thing she suspected of abducting her family was right here in front of her.

Neither Yahiro nor Himeka expected it would be this easy to find what they'd been searching for.

The Headless Rider. The living urban legend.

They couldn't even be sure it was actually *alive*.

Some said it was the vengeful spirit of a motorcycle rider who died in an accident.

Some said it was a reaper of the souls of the dead.

Some said it was a kind of fairy called a dullahan.

Some said it was just a piece of performance art.

Some said it was a spirit that had possessed a cursed motorcycle.

Some said it was some students playing a prank.

Some said it was a fake stunt from a television studio.

Some said it was an annoying piece of live art put on by an artist troupe.

Some said there was no such thing as the Headless Rider to begin with.

It was both a fantasy and an undeniable fact.

While they might have had some extraordinary qualities, the three teenagers were just that: teenagers. And now these ordinary kids were faced with this…*being*.

"No way...are you joking?" gasped Kuon, sweat breaking out on his brow.

Those words brought Yahiro's mind back to reality. "Is that...real?" he asked.

"What, do you need a fact-check or something?! Well, I suppose there were a number of fakes in the past..."

Yahiro glanced over at Himeka, who had regained her composure like normal but was also trembling, nearly imperceptibly.

For some reason, this helped him speak with a clarity that was so calm it surprised him.

"What now?"

"Huh?"

"Should we run away?"

"Uh..."

Some cool, collected words from her friend were just the thing to jolt Himeka into reason, too. "I'm fine. Thank you," she said, swallowing and slowing her breathing. She clenched her fists and silently stared at the approaching Headless Rider.

Kuon looked back and forth between Himeka and the rider and squawked, "Huh? Hey, wait a sec... Is it coming right for us? What should we do? If we're running, I'm running. But if we're talking, what do we say?"

He seemed slightly more comfortable than the other two, probably because he was from Tokyo and had been familiar with the Headless Rider's existence for years at this point.

But to Yahiro, it was just a fantastical urban legend, and to Himeka, it was the thing that had possibly stolen her sisters away from her.

Under those circumstances, there was one natural conclusion: It had come for the lone remaining sister.

Yahiro naturally found himself stepping forward in front of Himeka to protect her. At least that way, he would be ready, no matter what the Headless Rider did next.

Still, what do I do?

The sweat beaded up on Yahiro's forehead.

If it really attacks...can I fend it off?

He'd dealt with plenty of human opponents. For as frightening as the thug with the katana was, he'd managed to get past him safely.

But in all his life, he'd never faced off against a giant scythe fashioned out of writhing shadows. What if it started swinging around like in the videos online? How should he avoid it?

The mental image of what would happen if he *failed* sent a horrible shiver down Yahiro's back.

That instantly sharpened the concentration of the cowardly boy, revving his brain into maximum capacity and anticipating all possible situations to prepare for them.

But no sooner had it started than it stopped, just as quickly.

The action that the Headless Rider took next, barely six feet away from the teenagers, was completely outside of anything he was imagining.

"Um, excuse me."

Out of the riding suit so unreflective that it seemed to be made of pure darkness, the Headless Rider pulled out a smartphone, typed a rather anticlimactic sentence in Japanese, then turned the phone around to show them.

"Do you have a little time? I promise, I'm not trying to recruit you for some cult. I won't take long."

"   "
...
"   "
...
"...Huh?"

Kuon and Himeka were frozen in place. Yahiro's mind went momentarily blank.

It took several seconds before he realized that *he* was the one who had said something. Then, with a start, he reassessed what was happening around him.

The Headless Rider, that anomaly, had pulled out an undeniable tool of modern civilization: a smartphone.

Its smooth touch panel shone bright in the darkness, declaring its tiny presence. It seemed even brighter than usual because it was surrounded by unreflective pure blackness.

"Ummm..."

Yahiro still hadn't fully recovered from his prior assumption of an attack, and the thought occurred to him that this could just be a ruse to lure them into letting their guards down.

Cautiously, he asked, "Wh-what is it?"

"*Um, sorry, actually, I wanted to ask the girl there,*" the rider typed, rather matter-of-factly. The next message was "*Am I correct in assuming that you're Himeka Tatsugami?*"

"!"

She was shocked and briefly confused—but within a few seconds, she understood the implication of the question and glared with renewed wariness at the rider.

"Are…are my sisters all right?" she asked aggressively, assuming that this figure was either here to kidnap her next or to state the demands in exchange for freeing her sisters. "What…do you want?"

Her words suggested her default calmness, but Yahiro noticed there was just a slight tremble in her voice.

Still, the rider hastily waved a hand and showed them the screen from a distance.

"*I had a feeling you'd say that. Please don't get the wrong idea about me.*"

Apparently, the Headless Rider had anticipated their suspicion and was maintaining a distance of six feet. The figure increased the font size to facilitate easier communication at that range.

"*I'm very thankful that you didn't run away.*"

"…?"

"*I'll just state this first, for the record, that I am innocent of any abduction allegations,*" the Headless Rider typed, cutting right to the point.

The situation was about as suspicious as it could possibly be. The group just stared at one another without a word.

A bicycle just so happened to pass by at that moment, but at the sight of the inhuman creature, the longtime resident of Ikebukuro merely muttered, "Whoa! It's been a while," before continuing on his way.

All the tension had gone out of the scene. Himeka murmured, "No way…"

"*Yes way. I have no idea what's occurred with the kidnappings.*"

"That can't be true. My sisters…," she said, her voice hard but expression still the same. The Headless Rider's disarming, friendly attitude must have left her feeling more confusion than anger or fear.

"That's why I've come to see you, Himeka Tatsugami."

"Huh...?"

"Will you tell me more...about your sisters?"

And then, once again, the Headless Rider typed something they were not expecting to read.

"I want to help you rescue them."

A moment later, Kuon finally found his voice. "Hey, whoa, whoa, whoa! This doesn't make any sense!"

"Kuon?" Yahiro turned to him.

"Hey, c-c'mon, let's calm down! Everybody just chill out! Okay?"

"You're the one who's freaking out, Kuon."

Kuon ignored him and tried to put the situation into context. "What's the deal here? We were looking for the Headless Rider, right?! But it was actually watching for us and came to us first?!" Kuon was rambling on a mile a minute—probably due to anxiety. "And then it's like, 'Oh man, so it's true that if you go searching for the Headless Rider, you get kidnapped by the rider! We're done for! It's all over!' but then it pulls out its smartphone to talk to us?! And that's the newest model, too! Is this really the real Headless Rider?!"

"It's wearing clothes that don't reflect light, riding on a motorcycle with no engine noise. There's no room for doubt. No impostor is going to be able to get that kind of supernatural gear, and even if it was fake, the motorcycle seems legit. They'd have to be connected to the real thing and therefore worth talking to anyway."

"Wow, Yahiro, you're so rational it's kind of infuriating!" Kuon said, exasperated.

"..."

Yahiro didn't respond.

There it is again. It's that feeling I got...that Kuon is putting on an act of some kind.

He'd noticed the way his friend could act unnaturally at times, but he hadn't expected to feel it here and now, of all situations.

However, without understanding the point of it, Yahiro had no choice but to let it go for now.

"I'm glad you've decided to take me seriously," said the Headless Rider, who hadn't noticed anything strange from Kuon. It tilted its helmet into a quick bow, then showed the smartphone to Yahiro. *"Thank you. Are you local? You appear unfazed by my presence."*

"Actually, I'm not," Yahiro said, unable to bring himself to say that he had come all the way from Akita to see her.

What should I do? This isn't what I expected would happen.

In fact, the mental image he possessed of the Headless Rider had come completely crumbling to the ground from this experience. But then another memory flitted into his head.

Oh, hang on…I feel like this actually matches up with the way Akane and Mairu described the Headless Rider back at the dojo. Plus…

He also recalled what Shizuo Heiwajima said, feeling a twinge from the bruises that he thought had healed by now.

"She ain't the kind of person who abducts people and brings sorrow to the world."

That's right, he did say that. And if she's the way he described her, that would do a lot to explain this situation right now.

Yahiro felt he was close to finding the answers to all his questions, but Himeka was only getting more confused. She wasn't visibly fazed, thanks to her innately level personality, but that expressionless iron mask she wore still had tints of consternation in it right now.

"What are you saying? That you *didn't* kidnap my sisters…?"

"Well, it's the truth. I didn't do it. I don't have any proof of that, so you'll have to believe me."

"Then let's talk with the police about it."

"I can't deal with the police. I don't have a license. If I get arrested for these false charges, I'm in big trouble," the Headless Rider typed, looking momentarily deflated. *"Anyway, I want to rescue the people who've been abducted so that I can restore my honor. If there's someone posing as me out there, I need to catch them and bring them to justice."*

There was no way to see the Headless Rider's expression behind the helmet. In fact, there shouldn't be one at all.

But somehow, Yahiro felt like he could sense the passion behind the Headless Rider's text.

And above all else, the three teenagers shared one sentiment about the urban legend in the flesh: *She's…friendly. Surprisingly friendly!*

"Well, anyway, what is it you want from Tatsugami?" asked Yahiro, who had the most composure of the three. The Headless Rider's helmet tilted forward, and she started to type something.

However...

In the distance, there was a sound like a motorcycle engine revving, and then they could see something racing toward them at high speed.
"Huh?"
In fact, it was a line of three bikes front to back, weaving left and right like they were one long dragon as they rode down the street.
"A biker gang?"
The trio sidled over to the side of the alley, hoping to avoid any trouble as the bikers passed.

But instead, that seemed to be what the bikers were hoping for. The three motorcycles slowed down as they approached and stopped in a semicircle, blocking the teenagers against the wall.
The riders got off their wheels. The man in the lead looked to be about twenty years old, while the other two were young women.
At first glance, though, Yahiro thought all three of them were girls. When they pulled their helmets back to expose their faces, the man's features were so fine and beautiful that it was enough to fool Yahiro. His shining black hair was tied at the back of his head.
After a brief, cautious examination, the bone structure and slight bulge of the Adam's apple helped Yahiro identify the leader as a man, but the distinction was slight enough that it wasn't just him—plenty of people would make the same mistake.

"...Ugh!" Kuon grunted as he focused on a completely different detail about the trio.
There were distinctive stickers on all their vehicles. Stickers like white snake bones—but which on closer examination had arms and legs. The design of a dragon skeleton.
"It's Dragon Zombie..."

"That's correct," the man in the lead replied with a little chuckle.
The man had a dragon-themed tattoo around his neck, which was

a much more menacing complement to his delicate facial features. He did not look like an upstanding member of society.

The man glanced at the Headless Rider briefly before turning to Yahiro.

"?"

When he became aware of the man's gaze, Yahiro's hackles rose again.

Then the man turned to the women behind him and said lazily, "This one?"

"Yes. That's him, Libei."

"That's the boy," said each of the women in turn.

The man they called Libei grinned and looked at Yahiro again. "Good evening, then."

"Er...um, good evening," Yahiro said, bowing politely on instinct. He could hear Himeka murmur, "That's a man?" She must not have realized that until she heard his voice.

"It's nice to meet you. And to think that we encountered each other for the first time right in the presence of the Headless Rider. What a strange connection we've made."

He threw a glance at the rider again, sounding very casual. But he was about to send ice water through Yahiro's veins.

"I hear you're very strong."

"Huh?"

"Strong enough to beat Shizuo Heiwajima in a fight."

CHAPTER 5 B
The Mighty

Basement garage of Shinra's apartment—near Kawagoe Highway

It was several days earlier.

"I think you understand the situation now."
"...Yes."
In a corner of the empty garage, a man was speaking to a woman in a riding suit.
"Is there anything you'd like to say to me?"
"You have to believe me! I'm innocent!"
"I know you are. And I want to believe you."
The man was dressed in a suit and had a sharp gaze.
His name was Shiki. On paper, he was an art trader, but that was merely a public identity. His true nature was well known among people who lived in this neighborhood.
While he did not have visible tattoos or menacing battle scars, the air about him was dangerous enough that anyone with a keen enough eye could instantly tell he was in the business of organized crime.
In truth, he was Shiki, lieutenant of the Awakusu-kai under the Medei-gumi Syndicate. And he had been conducting business with the woman across from him for years.

"But you understand my point, don't you? If we're going to continue a fruitful business relationship, we'll need you to offer some kind of evidence of your innocence to the public."

"*Right.*"

"We can't have you under continual suspicion from the public, you see. That causes unwanted problems for us, being your business partner. We know you are entirely innocent and that everything you've suffered is unnecessary, but if we must, we will be forced to terminate our relationship with you."

Ordinarily, you would *want* to be free from any relationship with this man's organization. The woman in the riding suit had reasons for keeping that alive, though.

"That will mean we can no longer cover up any incidents involving you or offer you information in the future. Of course, we can't *physically* disappear you. But if push comes to shove, we could inform the police of your hideout and have them drive you out of town. I would like for us to work together in finding the truth so that it won't need to come to that."

It was harsh, even cruel, but the woman in the riding suit did not protest.

Shiki exhaled a deep breath, then resumed speaking, the edge in his voice lost.

"And on top of the business concerns, this is also a personal request."

"*Why is that?*"

"One of the kidnapped people is Miss Akane's friend."

"*!*"

"Miss Akane would be terribly hurt if she knew the one who saved her life was under suspicion... I hate to burden you with this just when you got back, but could you prioritize this over your usual work?"

The woman in the riding suit leaned forward, her helmet dipping down.

The man from the underworld saw it and chuckled to himself, turning his back. "Thank you. I'll send all the information we have to Dr. Kishitani by e-mail. I'm praying that we can continue to patronize the services both of you offer."

Shiki did not live in the light. He was part of the world that twisted the ethics of society with power of all kinds, not least of which was violence. It was how he made a living.

But compared to him, the woman's place in society was even more extreme.

Because she was an urban legend who struggled to live in human society—though she herself was not human. She was the Headless Rider.

♂♀

No, Celty Sturluson was not human.

She was a type of fairy commonly known as a dullahan, found from Scotland to Ireland—a being that visited the homes of those close to death to inform them of their impending deaths.

The dullahan carried its own severed head under its arm, rode on a two-wheeled carriage called a Cóiste Bodhar pulled by a headless horse, and approached the homes of the soon to die.

Anyone foolish enough to open the door was drenched with a basin full of blood. Thus, the dullahan, like the banshee, made its name as a herald of ill fortune throughout European folklore.

But her background and nature didn't matter anymore.

Because now, she was under suspicion of something she had nothing to do with—and people were starting to think of her as the "Reaper of Abduction."

♂♀

Shinra's apartment—near Kawagoe Highway

Thirty minutes after her conversation with Shiki, the Headless Rider, Celty Sturluson, curled into a gloomy little ball in her apartment. It was bad enough being suspected of kidnapping, but the story had also taken over the Internet so thoroughly that it was basically treated as fact.

As she hugged her knees on the sofa, Celty's live-in partner, the unlicensed doctor Shinra Kishitani, sighed. "I'm telling you, Celty. You shouldn't let this bother you."

"It's impossible for me not to be bothered by this. My reputation's been completely obliterated."

Not only had both true and false stories about her spread all over the Internet, but people even lobbied insults at her like, "I bet the inside of that helmet is stuffed with kelp stalks," which was rude to both Celty *and* kelp stalks. The whole ordeal had left her reeling.

"Why kelp stalks…?"

"It's all right. I'll ask my super-hacker friend to go after the people slandering you online, and then I'll slice them in two like actual kelp stalks."

"Super-hacker? Are you serious…?"

"I just recently got in touch with him online. He can find out all kinds of details about people. His name's Tsukumoya. Anyway, he'll be able to identify the people who are writing crap about you. I'll ask him to hack their computers, grab their downloaded porn videos, then send them to their workplaces and schools."

Celty ignored Shinra's revenge plan—which seemed designed mostly to cause trouble for those workplaces and schools—and clenched her fists. She bolted to her feet.

"Argh! Forget about revenge. We have to start by correcting their mistake… And I'm worried for those who are missing."

"You're more worried for others than your own reputation? Why, Celty, your compassion is unrivaled in quantity and quality!"

"Whatever. Do we have any clues?"

"Hmm. Mr. Shiki sent me an e-mail with some materials attached. It seems that the Awakusu-kai are doing some research on their own," Shinra said, scrolling down the screen of the laptop set up on the table. "Of the recent disappearances, there's a lot of attention being paid to the two sisters who vanished. And the older of the two was a tabloid writer who was doing some research on you, Celty."

"On me?"

"Yes. Umm…looks like there are three sisters, and it was the eldest and youngest who disappeared."

"What about the second?" Celty typed, a natural question.

"She's not mentioned here," Shinra replied, "so she must be all right. But if we find out why *she* wasn't abducted, maybe that will be a big hint. Though I'm sure the police have been looking into that already..."

"*Hmm... And we don't know anyone at the police we could ask for information... Oh, I know! Do you think that super-hacker of yours could peek at the police files for—,*" Celty typed, then smacked the back of her own neck to scold herself. "*Argh, no! No! What's the point of asking people to commit crimes in order to solve a crime? I'm being stupid!*"

"That's a funny thing to hear you say after running illegal courier jobs without a license or a headlight. But it's also what I love about you... Anyway, it'll be fine, Celty. The quandary of whether to peek or not is irrelevant; investigations like that don't take part on externally accessible computers anyway, to protect against leaks."

"*Oh, that makes sense. But then...what should we do?*"

"According to Mr. Shiki's information, the middle sister is a student at Raira Academy."

Raira Academy.

The mention of that name gave her pause. Ever since its premerger days as Raijin High, Celty had deep connections to that particular school.

She'd never worn the uniform, of course, but many of the people whom Celty knew well had gone through that school. She even knew a couple of currently enrolled students there. Of all the schools that existed in Japan, it was easily the closest to her in terms of personal connections.

"Well, that's convenient. Ryuugamine's still there as a senior, since he was held back a year during his hospitalization."

Ryuugamine.

Another name that was very familiar to Celty, nearly as much as Raira Academy.

Mikado Ryuugamine was a third-year student at Raira. He should have graduated already, but he'd suffered a terrible stab wound to the stomach and had to be hospitalized for a lengthy time. The ordeal forced him to repeat a school year.

"Let's have him get in touch for us."

"*Wait, Shinra.*" Celty grabbed his hand before he could pick up his phone and start typing. "*I don't want to get Mikado involved in this.*"

"Celty…"

"His life is finally peaceful again. I still think of him as a friend, and that's exactly why I don't want to pressure him into getting into this dark, dangerous business."

"You're so sweet, Celty. I almost feel jealous of Mikado," Shinra teased.

Celty kindly, gently typed, *"Yes, you're the only one I want to involve in dark, dangerous business, Shinra."*

She meant it to be half-sardonic, but Shinra's eyes lit up like a child's who had just been given a new toy, and he clung to her.

"Celty! Oh, Celty! That means we're always one and the same! One in the hand, two in the bush, three's company, four's a—*mrblmrbgh!*"

"Argh, now's not the time for this!"

She grabbed a handful of Shinra's cheek to peel his face off her, but he was still delighted.

"That's better. Now there's the Celty I know."

"Anyway, there has to be someone better than Mikado for this. Someone who's meant for jobs like this! Someone who's spent a lot of time manipulating us!"

"Who, Izaya? He's still missing," Shinra pointed out.

Celty typed, *"Aoba, obviously! Aoba Kuronuma!"*

"Ohhh…"

Shinra's expression darkened slightly.

He clearly didn't think highly of the boy. He took a deep breath, exhaled, then grabbed his phone.

"If you ask me, he only saw you as a tool to be manipulated to his own ends, so I think he deserves to take on a huge debt from seedy loan sharks, require drastic collection methods, and simply vanish off the face of the earth."

"Wow, that took a dark turn."

In the time that took, the call went through, and Shinra growled, "Ah…is that you, Kuronuma? Listen, you're not my first choice, but I need your help for something. I want you to look for a student at Raira Academy and send their information back to me.

"Let's see…all I know is that her name is Himeka Tatsugami."

♂♀

Ikebukuro—present day

That was how, through Aoba's help, Celty Sturluson had come into possession of a picture of Himeka Tatsugami, which helped her locate the girl in person on the street.

It took just a few days for her to find the girl, based on nothing but the clue that she was walking around with a green-haired boy. However, since the discussion wasn't really meant for a public setting, she had to trail them until they headed down this secluded alley before she could approach them.

I would have preferred to talk with her alone, but I suppose she might have run away if I scared her too much.

Celty's supposition was correct; the boys with her were keeping her calm and capable of holding a conversation.

First things first—I need to clear up the misunderstanding...

Her idea was to prove that she was innocent beyond a doubt via the alibi of her vacation videos.

If only the Dragon Zombie riders hadn't shown up to interrupt them.

"Very nice to meet you," said the beautiful young man with the soothing smile.

That was enough to instantly tell Celty what she needed to know: His was a face she had seen years ago, although she'd never talked to him.

Libei. He's back in town.

Libei Ying.

The Taiwanese expat once led the biker gang known as Dragon Zombie, splitting control over Ikebukuro with Jan-Jaka-Jan. In order to treat an illness, he traveled back to Taiwan to see his doctor. Apparently, he was back in Ikebukuro now.

I've heard from Izaya that he shares ancestors with the Ying family in the Chinese mafia. But apparently, it's a distant relation back in China, so who knows if he actually has connections to call upon...

So why was this man here now?

If he wanted a fight, he probably would have brought more people with him; two women stood beside him.

Though maybe these two are each as tough as Mikage from Rakuei Gym...

Celty was frozen, unable to decide what this situation meant. Libei used that opportunity to turn away from her and spoke to the boy standing next to Himeka Tatsugami.

"I hear you're very strong."

"Huh?" Yahiro blurted out.

"Strong enough to beat Shizuo Heiwajima in a fight."

...

Huh?

What did he just say?

That was a strange combination of words she thought she'd heard. A totally illogical combination, in fact—the subject, verb, and object made no sense like this.

It was as if someone had just said, "The sun's so cold." She had to stay silent and listen on, just to make sure she hadn't misheard.

Meanwhile, totally ignorant of the Headless Rider's mental gymnastics, Libei introduced himself to the young man.

"I'm Libei. Libei Ying. Nice to meet you," he said, smiling easily and offering his hand.

The boy looked taken aback but accepted the handshake. "Uh, hi... I'm Yahiro Mizuchi."

"First things first, I need to apologize. Sorry, okay?"

"Huh?"

"I'm going to give you a little *test* now."

In the next moment, Yahiro Mizuchi's world turned upside down.

"?!"

Yahiro instantly understood what had happened to him.

His center of gravity had instantly been thrown off from the handshake, and a powerful leg sweep toppled him sideways.

But even before his mind recognized this, Yahiro's body reacted on pure instinct.

*   *   *

Attacked.   *By who?*   *Why?*
    Sudden.   *But I did nothing.*
  Scared.   *Scared, scared, scared.*   *Hurry.*
Gotta beat him quickly.   *Before I get hurt.*   *Before I get hurt.*
  Before I get hurt. Before I get hurt, before I get hurt, before I get hurt!

All of these thoughts shot through his mind in a fraction of a second, and without any time lag, Yahiro's body launched a counterattack at his *enemy.*

Before his body, rotating in the air, could fall to the ground, he shot his hand out below him. Holding up his entire body with the strength of one forearm, he twisted his body and tangled his legs around Libei's neck.

"Oh?"

Libei failed to anticipate this maneuver. He expected more of a capoeira move, a handstand into a side kick.

Instead, the legs tangled around his neck and threatened to pull him down sideways. Libei managed to slip free at the last possible moment, however, and retreated a step to restore his balance.

Meanwhile, Yahiro managed to utilize his momentum to his advantage as well and was already on his feet again. He promptly rushed forward, glaring at Libei with eyes like a bird of prey's, keeping his balance low as he rushed across the asphalt.

Libei lifted his leg for a knee kick against his opponent, who'd started his dash from a crouch. But Yahiro either read that move ahead of time or exhibited superhuman reflexes, because he lifted himself upright and jumped just before contact.

Thud. His right foot landed on Libei's knee, and he launched himself off it for greater height.

His target was the other man's face.

A vicious knee headed straight for the bridge of Libei's nose—but the biker twisted out of the way just in time to avoid the blow.

"...!"

Yahiro's posture shifted in midair as he reached for his opponent's neck. If he grabbed it, he could choke out the enemy. In fact, the sheer momentum of the fall alone would probably break his neck.

"Yaaah!"

Libei rolled sideways to escape from Yahiro's hands. He hurried back to his feet, but Yahiro was already approaching again.

"...!"

A palm strike rushed toward Libei's jaw from a lower diagonal.

The moment he evaded it, a hammer blow of the bottom of Yahiro's fist rushed down toward his brow.

"Wai..."

Libei just barely avoided contact. Because he was successfully evading each strike, it might seem to a passive observer that Libei was quite a capable fighter.

But in truth, he was feeling the pressure.

Ever since his initial ambush attack was blocked, he'd been completely on the defensive. There wasn't even an opening for him to try countering.

Y-yikes...

And it wasn't like the younger boy was simply swinging as hard as he could at Libei. The alternation between the base of the hand and clenched fists was enough to make clear he knew what he was doing.

Libei tried to put more distance between them, but Yahiro just pushed even closer. He got so close it would be considered a clinch in boxing—no room for either person to take a proper swing—and curled his body.

A tightly folded elbow darted forward at Libei's jaw like a sharp blade. Libei swayed out of the way—but the other arm lunged for his throat from the other direction, as though waiting for that cue.

Libei swiped it back with his right, but it felt to him like he was doomed. It seemed like every one of Yahiro's attacks was coming at full power, and he lunged for Libei's vital points without mercy or hesitation. And despite the constant rush of attacks, Yahiro didn't seem to be tiring in the least.

No doubt about it—he's strong! But it's different from Shizuo Heiwajima!

How much stamina did he have? Libei couldn't even catch a breath to analyze the secrets of his opponent's strength.

I figured people were exaggerating when they said he nearly beat Shizuo...but now I believe it! What a strange kid.

Libei stared at Yahiro's eyes. What he saw there, through the narrowed slits of Yahiro's lids, gave rise to doubt.

Why...why do you look so terrified when you're the one overpowering me?

Despite his desperate defensive gambit, he felt himself grin—a crucial mistake.

Yahiro's leg came swinging up at the gap between his legs.

Uh-oh!

His hands jutted downward to stop the kick just before it could strike, but that was just a feint from Yahiro. With Libei lunging forward to block the kick, Yahiro was able to use both hands to grab his jaw and the back of his head.

Then the kid twisted and pushed Libei toward the ground.

An unwise act of resistance could easily break Libei's neck. His instincts cut off all resistance, and he allowed himself to be taken to the ground to ensure he didn't snap his neck struggling.

The hands immediately came off his face, and he saw Yahiro's ankle lift off the ground.

Uh-oh, that's not good.

All the hair on his body stood on end when he realized the foot was going to stomp directly on his own face.

I'm about to die...

As Libei's life began to flash before his eyes a dark shadow crossed in front of them.

"?!"

"!"

Everyone present was stunned, not only Yahiro and Libei.

The Headless Rider sent out a shadow that split the space between Libei on the ground and Yahiro standing over him, reaching for the foot that was about to plunge downward.

"...!"

Yahiro immediately changed direction to avoid the shadow coming to tangle up his foot, and he bounded backward. Once, twice—even that wasn't enough—Yahiro backed away, jump by jump, like a shrimp fleeing in water.

Once he'd backed away to a distance about as long as the street was wide, he stopped and cast a wary glare at Celty, the source of the shadow.

Incredible.
For her part, Celty marveled at Yahiro's physical capabilities.
I didn't expect he'd actually slip away from me.
She just wanted to stop the sudden fight that broke out, and as Yahiro was the one doing all the attacking, she thought that immobilizing him was the quickest way.

But when she extended her shadow to grab him, the way she'd caught street thugs so many times, Yahiro reacted with all the speed and instinct of a wild animal.

Does this mean...he really can beat Shizuo? Did something happen between them? What went on here in the last six months...?
Celty could only imagine how the city had changed in the time she was gone. She didn't realize all this had happened in just the last few days.

But aside from that, her suspicions weren't that far off. She watched Libei getting back up off the ground and considered further.

The last time he was in Ikebukuro, he was a cause of concern to Kadota and Izaya, wasn't he? And he got pushed around this easily...
What's going on? Who is that boy?
Yahiro seemed like an average kid. He wasn't as weak as Mikado, but he was hardly some powerful, muscled giant. She couldn't tell what his muscles were like beneath his school uniform, but in terms of fighting styles, he was probably built more like a swift boxer than a bulky wrestler or judoka.

There was no end to the questions, but most important of all right now was to stop this fight from continuing.

How do I do that? Swallow him up whole in shadow? That feels like it'll be a bit too involved... I can't remember anyone evading my shadow so skillfully since that motorcycle cop.
A shiver ran down Celty's back at the thought of the traffic cop, her mortal nemesis.

Fortunately, she didn't need to wonder what to do for much longer.

The boy with the dyed green hair called out, "Hey! Yahiro! Yahiro! Chill out, man! C'mon!"

There was a slight shift in the look in Yahiro's eyes.

"Ah…"

Then his head spun around. He glanced about, then down at his hands and feet. Suddenly, his expression was mournful, no longer feral and defensive.

The green-haired boy rushed over to him. "Get a grip, man! It was over! You won, okay? Yeah, whoo-hoo! My hero!"

"…"

But Yahiro hardly seemed to hear the half-ironic cheers from his friend.

Elsewhere, the two women accompanying the young man were tending to him.

"Didn't we warn you? You can't go in *unarmed*."

"This is what you get for being cocky," they scolded Libei.

He shrugged and said, "Look, I'm sorry, Big Sis. You two were right."

That response bowled Celty over.

…Big Sis? Wait…both of them?!

The two women on either side of him looked so young. Barely more than girls.

"Did you just say 'Big Sis'?" asked the green-haired boy; Celty wasn't the only one who'd caught that.

"Yep, sure did. You might not believe it, but we're siblings. I'm twenty-one."

"Twenty-two."

"And I'm twenty-three," finished the girls, waving their hands.

"Huh? Uh, okay. W-well, hi, I'm Kuon Kotonami," he said, flustered into introducing himself.

Yahiro was watching Libei with concerned caution. "Um…I…"

But Libei cut him off. "Sorry about all that. Let's just say I lost, the fight's over, and we've all made up. Okay?" He smiled breezily, as though his face hadn't been in danger of being crushed just moments earlier.

"Uh, sure…I went way overboard. I'm sorry," Yahiro said, deflated. He bowed, and Celty finally felt relieved.

Is it…over, then? That's good.

At last, she would be able to proceed with what she wanted to talk

about. She turned to Himeka, who had watched the whole altercation play out in mute shock, and typed some more on her smartphone.

"Well, that was more exciting than necessary, but I'm glad your friend didn't get hurt."

In the release of tension following the fight, Celty found her typing was a little more informal than before.

"Can I help you search for your missing family?"

♂♀

At that moment, intersection

"Whoa, whoa, whoa… What the hell just happened there?"

At an intersection not far away from the Headless Rider, some snoops were spying on the scene from around the corner.

"Holy shit, Mr. Horada! I can't believe the Headless Rider's involved, too!"

"Sh-shuddup! Don't be afraid of that fraud! The *real* problem is that Dragon Zombie's involved in this, obviously!"

"Do you think the guy who was just fighting with Libei Ying was the same guy who fought Shizuo?"

"Probably. You saw how he moved, right? He treated Libei Ying like a little kid, even if he doesn't have that Blue Dragon Sword with him today," Horada said breathlessly. He and his followers were watching Yahiro from a distance.

They had spotted the green-haired boy from the now-famous video and spent thirty minutes following him from a distance. They could have rushed in and demanded to know where that guy was—but they had to be careful, because the person they were searching for was mighty enough to stand toe to toe with Shizuo. If the boy with him was the guy they were searching for and the questioning made him angry, he could have started throwing fists at them instead.

While they mulled over what to do, the situation took a few strange turns. First, the Headless Rider, Horada's nemesis, showed up to accost them. Then, within minutes, the leader of Dragon Zombie showed up with some women in tow.

A fight broke out, then ended as soon as it began, once the Headless Rider intervened to pull them apart.

But Horada's group was too far away to hear what they had been talking about since then.

"This looks bad, Mr. Horada. I have a feeling Dragon Zombie's gonna scoop up that kid before we can."

"Don't be stupid—they were just fighting!"

"Yeah, but they seem to have made up already."

"What?!"

Horada poked his head around the corner and saw that the hostilities seemed to be over. They were all gathered together on the side of the road.

"Damn...gotta do something," he muttered. A disgusting leer crawled over his face. "Let's change targets, then. First, let's work on his little friend."

"The green-haired guy?"

"You bet. You know what they say, 'If you want the horse, first shoot the merchant.'"

"I've never heard anyone say that... Are you sure that's a thing?" asked one of his henchmen.

Horada ignored him and focused on the other student in the group. "Plus, it's hard to see from this distance..."

His tongue flicked out to wet his lips as he stared at the girl with the long black hair.

"But that girl looks like she's totally my type... No harm in gettin' to know her, right?"

$$\male\female$$

Alleyway

"I...cannot entirely trust you," Himeka told Celty impassively, having listened to the entire story.

"I completely understand. But I don't have any way to prove my innocence other than giving an alibi."

"But...I will take your help. For the sake of my sisters."

"*You will?! Thank you!*"

"Well, it's helping us. So I'm grateful," Himeka said, bowing.

Yahiro found it impossible to tell how she was reacting at a glance. Himeka was not the kind of person who displayed much emotion, so you didn't need to be a socially withdrawn person like Yahiro to find her hard to read.

"This is a very interesting story," commented Libei, who'd been listening in on their conversation. "I'll let you know if I learn anything, too. Would you mind if I ask for your numbers?" he asked Yahiro and Himeka casually.

Celty was mystified by this. "*Why? Dragon Zombie doesn't have any connection to this, right?*"

"Look, I just want people to owe me favors. I get it if you don't want to be involved with a biker gang, but you need all the help you can get, don't you?"

"But I..."

"Are you still angry about me starting a fight with you out of nowhere?"

Yahiro shook his head vigorously. "No, it's my fault for getting carried away... I'm sorry about that."

"Nah, it's fine! Say, here's a question: Do you like motorcycles? Think this riding suit looks pretty hot?"

"Ah, er, I guess...," Yahiro stammered. He didn't actually understand what was being asked of him.

Libei chuckled and asked him directly this time. "You wanna join our gang? We're the Dragon Zombies."

"Gang?" Yahiro repeated, confused.

Kuon hurried to interject. "Okay, okay, okay! Sorry about him—he just moved here from Akita. He doesn't know how things work in Ikebukuro... Plus, he's a good fighter, but he's also a very good kid who keeps his nose clean. He's not really cut out to be a biker."

"That's nice, but I wasn't asking you..."

Libei gave Kuon a rather piercing stare, thought it over, then said to Yahiro, "Well, I suppose he's right. I'm not going to force you to make a decision. As an apology for what I did today, I'll make it up to you later. Let's keep this relationship fifty-fifty."

"Fifty-fifty?"

"Yeah. One side needs help with something, they ask the other, then help out in return... That kinda thing. I'm not gonna ask you to do anything crazy like 'die' or 'hand over your girl.'"

Libei then turned to Celty.

"I'd like to do the same with you, too. What do you say?"

"I don't mind, but the only thing I can give you is my e-mail address," Celty replied, immediately agreeing to trade contact information with him. She must have been impressed by how normally he was treating her.

"That's enough for me. You're friends with Shizuo Heiwajima and Izaya Orihara, aren't you? I was always jealous of them for getting to be friends with an urban legend."

"I'm not friends with Izaya...," she protested.

Kuon leaned in and said, "Um...Miss Headless Rider...? Er, should I call you Celty instead?"

"Yes, what is it?"

"Um, I don't mean to be rude, but can I take a picture with you? No need for contact info."

"I don't mind..."

As soon as he saw the acceptance on her screen, Kuon immediately lined up next to Celty and used his phone to take a selfie with the both of them. Once he'd gotten a few, he suddenly became extraordinarily excited.

"Whoo-hoo! Thank you! Can I put these on my blog and stuff?"

"Wow, you're really aggressive. But...I don't mind. Just watch out, because the cops and other weirdos will come after you."

It wasn't a big problem for Celty, who was used to people taking photos of her. She was more worried about the potential effects on the people who took them.

"Nah, it's fine, I already know about that. And I can rely on a good friend for help if I need it."

"Oh, Mr. Kuronuma?" said Yahiro.

"Huh? Sorry, what name was that?"

"Whoops! Look out—people are starting to notice us!" said Kuon, hurriedly changing the topic the moment Celty heard the familiar name.

It was true that the number of lookie-loos in the distance was growing. The Headless Rider wasn't a rare sight to the people of Ikebukuro anymore, but there were tourists from elsewhere who had succumbed to curiosity and taken their cameras out.

"Er, sorry. I'll contact you later for more details."

Celty didn't want to cause more trouble for Himeka and her friends, so she finished up exchanging details and got back onto her black motorcycle.

"Thank you. If I learn anything, I will get in touch."

♂♀

Shopping district, Ikebukuro

The gathering split up, and Kuon went home first, claiming he remembered an errand he needed to run. Yahiro decided to head back to the station with Himeka.

For a while, neither of them spoke. But Himeka could see that he was looking for something to say and failing, and she mercifully broke the silence.

"That was surprising. I didn't know you were so good at fighting."

"Oh, th-that? Um…"

"It's fine if you don't want to talk about it. I won't be bothered," she said flatly.

Yahiro worried that he had frightened her with that combat display. In an attempt to diffuse the tension, he changed the topic and said, "The Headless Rider seems pretty nice."

"…Yes, I suppose," Himeka replied without emotion.

"It's all right now," he went on. "With the real thing helping out, I'm sure we'll find your sisters."

He meant it to be reassuring to her, but as usual, Himeka did not seem to react in any way. She just stared into the distance and murmured mostly to herself, "Even still…I think the Headless Rider is a demon."

"Huh? What do you mean?" he asked skeptically.

She didn't turn back to look at him. "She won't even let me hate her for no good reason…"

It wasn't an answer to his question. It was like she was talking to herself.

♂♀

Shinra's apartment near Kawagoe Highway—three AM

"Welcome home, Celty!"

"I'm back. Sorry about being so late. I was looking into things all over and lost track of time."

At the moment she showed her smartphone screen to Shinra, he rushed to embrace her.

"Oh, I'm so glad you're all right!"

"Let go. What do you mean, glad I'm all right?"

Normally, she would pull him off as soon as he did this, but something about his concern for her safety struck her as odd.

"Did something happen?"

"Something definitely did happen. It seems like this case is a lot more dangerous than we're giving it credit for."

"What do you mean?" she asked, quite serious. Shinra finally pulled away and took on a dead serious manner that was very out of character.

The answer was something she found difficult to believe.

"I just received a call from Mr. Akabayashi...

"He says they can't reach Mr. Shiki..."

INTERMISSION
Online Rumors (4)

On the Ikebukuro information site IkeNew! Version I.KEBU.KUR.O

```
Popular Post: [In a Different Sense]
The Headless Rider being super-friendly
[Urban legend is over]
```

"I'm friends with the Headless Rider now." (Rehosted from a personal blog)

Guess what? I ran into the Headless Rider in Ikebukuro today!
She was actually really cool!
She's really down-to-earth and even let me take a picture with her!
Her favorite food is castella cake bites, and her favorite idol is Yuuhei Hanejima!
It was so much fun. We talked about the latest shows and even went out to karaoke. I heard so many stories!
I'm amazed.
I'm getting the chills just remembering it.
After meeting her in person, I'd say she's just really normal.
Apparently, she even reads manga. She's just like everybody else.
She said she won a raffle from a store and was on a vacation to Hawaii for the last six months!

That counts as an alibi, right?

I mean, how could you be abducting people from Hawaii?

She feels really awful about all these weird rumors about her!

Anyway, I can totally brag to my friends about this.

Maybe I should introduce her to all of them, too.

Wouldn't it be crazy if we made a club to protect the Headless Rider?

—(Original blog post has been deleted)

Comment from IkeNew! *Administrator*

Making friends immediately after returning, she is.

What was that whole abduction controversy about...?

This boy put all kinds of personal information up online, including a photograph—but abducted, he isn't.

If he doesn't vanish, then the urban legend of the Headless Rider being a kidnapper will have no legs, in the end.

How does it feel to be tricked by false stories? Feel foolish, do you?

A very normal person, the Headless Rider is.

Skeptical that there is really nothing under that helmet now, I am.

If a proper legal identity she has, eligible to sue for defamation, she is. Though arrested first for traffic violations, she likely will be.

By the way, a privacy bar over the boy's face to protect his identity, I've placed.

Although many green-haired teens there are in Japan, I doubt.

And complain and bash all you want, stop talking like Yoda I will not.

Against the slanderers of speech quirks and character building, I will fight.

Admin: Rira Tailtooth Zaiya

A selection of representative twits from the social network Twittia

57

They sound like they're really good friends.

> →The rider was usually friendly, right? Had people riding on the bike a lot.

> →What's up with this article? IkeNew was the site spreading all those rumors in the first place.

> →They never apologize for running false rumors. That's just their style.

Turn her in to the police!

> →We don't know that she actually kidnapped anyone.

> →No, for riding without headlights.

> →Oh, that. Good point.

I don't know—do you suppose the Headless Rider really isn't the culprit after all?

So the question becomes, Who's really responsible for the kidnappings?

If the people who vanished were chasing the Headless Rider, maybe it's someone who bears a grudge against the rider.

> →Why would you kidnap people because you had a grudge?

> →To pin the crime on the rider, right?

> →Hell of a grudge.

> →I'm guessing those victims are never coming back, huh?

> →Oh, right. If they show up alive, they'll be able to prove the rider's innocence.

> →May they rest in peace.

> →That's really inappropriate.

> →Sorry.

This "Headless Rider" is a fake. Stop spreading this article.

→Looks real to me. The suit isn't reflecting any light.

→You can do anything with a computer. It's fake.

→Is there a reason you don't want it to be real?

→Blocked.

→What? Just for that?

→So desperate…

→I bet this person really is trying to keep people from thinking it's real.

→What if he's the real kidnapper?

*(The original poster deleted their account.)

Where's the original blog this came from? I can't find it in a search.

→Good question.

→It was probably the right call to delete it. Don't want to get in trouble with school.

→I've seen that guy around a lot in Ikebukuro lately.

→Yeah, he's got really crazy hair.

→He hangs out with the Blue Squares, too.

→Wait, they're still around?

→Yup. Meanwhile, the Dollars totally vanished.

→Dollars? Was that a gang?

→You serious? It's only been two years.

→Look, I don't keep track of what the motorcycle gangs are called.

→Not a motorcycle gang, a street gang!

I hope that isn't the real Headless Rider.

→Why not?

→It's kind of disappointing, learning that they're just a normal person.

→Just think about it scientifically. It's impossible.

→You might think so, but let me dream, ok?

→What if it's a supernatural phenomenon you can have a conversation with?

→I don't know, it's like finding out that the idol you like wears dorky clothes in private...

→What's wrong with wearing dorky clothes in private?

At the convenience store just now, I saw the boy with the green hair who was in the picture with the Headless Rider.

→Which store?

→I don't know if I should answer publicly. If you follow me, I can send you a DM.

→Followed.

(No more public twits after this point.)

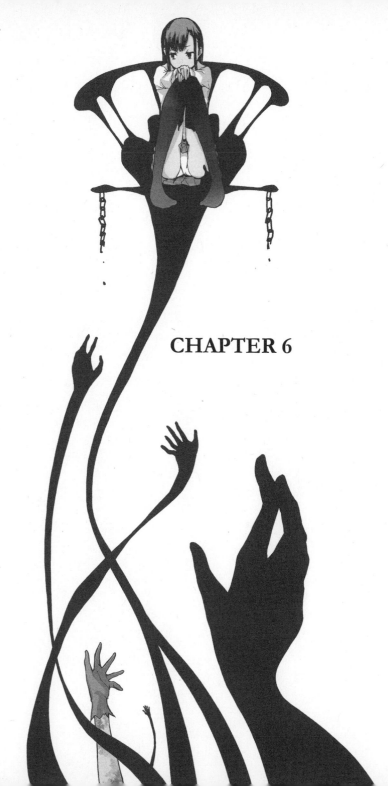

CHAPTER 6

CHAPTER 6 A
The Guests

The next day—Raira Academy

"Morning."

"…Good morning."

Himeka's response to Yahiro was the same as ever.

"Yesterday was really something, wasn't it?" he said.

"Yes. I'm still having trouble processing it."

"…"

He thought about asking her what she meant with her last words the day before, but he decided that it would probably be more invasive than necessary, so he hesitated.

"Do you still think the Headless Rider is a demon?" he asked anyway, despite his misgivings. If he were a more considerate person than he was, Yahiro's childhood would have gone much better.

"…You're very persistent," Himeka noted, but she didn't seem to be that upset, either. Most likely, their interactions over the last few days had taught her a bit about him. "Perhaps this would be easier to understand if the Headless Rider was the culprit, like I had assumed."

"But if the person who did it uses strange shadows like she does, I don't think we'd ever get back the people who were taken."

"That's true. You've got a point," Himeka said brusquely.

Yahiro wasn't sure how to respond. "In that case…"

"But the thing is, Yahiro, I don't think that's exactly it."

"Huh?"

She faced forward as she walked, speaking briskly. "If the Headless Rider is this friendly, then wouldn't it make her that much more approachable to the people who have been studying her?"

"Ah..."

"They could talk to her in a secluded place or the mountains in the middle of nowhere."

"I guess...that makes sense."

He felt like he understood her argument. At any rate, it was clear she still suspected the rider of something.

Yahiro didn't think her opinion of the rider as a "demon" was something that came from such a simplistic suspicion, though.

Hmm... What should I say? I'm so awkward in these situations. I'm sure Kuon would be able to ask the right questions to reach the answer, but that's just 'cause he's so sociable. I wish I was as good at talking to people as he is.

His characterization of Kuon as "sociable" was an interesting one, given the boy's use of bold green hair to intimidate people and keep them away.

Yahiro and Himeka headed to the classroom without digging any deeper into the topic.

Only when homeroom started did they notice what was wrong.

That familiar green head was nowhere to be found in the classroom.

Huh? Is he staying home today?

It was possible that he was simply tardy, but after what happened yesterday, Yahiro couldn't hide the disquieting feeling in his heart.

When first period ended and they went on break, Yahiro tried calling Kuon's phone.

"The number you have dialed is not currently available," said the electronic woman's voice on the line, which only made the foreboding worse.

Then Yahiro remembered about the call Kuon made to him last night and the things his friend had said.

"Yo. That was pretty wild back there.

"I gotta say, Himeka is more low-key than I expected.

"It's like...I thought she was gonna jump on the Headless Rider and scream, Give back my sisters! but fortunately she was keeping it together way better.

"Anyway, tomorrow I'll start hitting up people who might have a grudge against the rider.

"See ya at school. I'm going out to the convenience store for a sec."

They had talked about some other things, but he remembered that the rest of the conversation wasn't important.

The point was, he said he'd come to school. It was hard to imagine that Kuon was cutting classes.

Yahiro felt a shiver run down his spine. One of the rumors surrounding the Headless Rider and the disappearances had popped into his mind.

Those who chase after the Headless Rider vanish first.

Given what happened with Himeka's sisters, it was a very believable rumor.

But no. Wait. That doesn't make sense.

In that case, Tatsugami and I should have gone missing first.

At this point, Yahiro was completely at a loss. As class resumed, his worry remained.

During lunch break, he decided to talk to Himeka about it.

"What do you think happened to Kuon?"

"He's probably ditching. He doesn't seem like an honor student to me."

"That's pretty cold... Anyway, I still can't reach his phone."

"If he's not ditching...then maybe the Headless Rider had something to do with it," Himeka said boldly, her expression darkening a bit.

"I don't want to believe that's true...but I guess I can send her a text," Yahiro suggested, starting up the e-mail app he'd learned how to use for contacting his family back home.

But before his fingers could start typing, a new voice said, "Hey, Mizuchi and Tatsugami, are you going out?"

It was one of the girls in the class, who had noticed that the two were always hanging out.

"No. We're just together a lot," Himeka said bluntly. Her tone wasn't disgusted or shy, just bluntly honest about the facts.

"Really? Is that true, Yahiro?"

"Huh? Why are you asking me?" His own blunt honesty was no less impressive than Himeka's. "I'd be really happy if I had a girlfriend as pretty as her. But we're not going out."

"Wow, you practically asked her out just now!"

"What? Did I?"

"Yes! That's hilarious!"

Yahiro was confused, but the girls decided he had to have been joking and started howling with laughter.

"C'mon, Himeka, you could stand to be more bashful about it!"

"Isn't Yahiro really funny?"

"Are all people in Akita like you?"

"No, definitely not," he said. He was on solid ground with that question, at least.

He was different from the people back home: They were normal, and according to them, he was a monster. Yahiro's view of this was rather unfair to himself.

Meanwhile, the girls asked, "But you're also always hanging out with that green-haired boy. Kotonami, right?"

"What's up with that? A love triangle?"

"Is he your favorite, Tatsugami?" the girls chattered.

But Himeka just said, "No. We're just together a lot, same as with him."

"Oh my God, it's like you're bragging or something!" The girls laughed, teasing.

Himeka didn't seem affected by it at all—but the next innocent thing they said elicited a minor reaction from her.

It did the same for Yahiro.

"But speaking of Kotonami, do you think his story about the Headless Rider is true?"

"Huh?" both Yahiro and Himeka said together, turning their heads.

"What, you didn't know? It was all people were talking about between periods," said the girl, taking out her smartphone to show them. "Here...isn't that Kotonami there in the news?"

On the screen was a picture of the Headless Rider with a young man, a black bar obscuring his eyes.

But the bar was rendered completely pointless by the bright green hair visible above it. And that was how, by the middle of the day, Yahiro and Himeka at last understood what was going on.

Kuon Kotonami had become the newest gossip.

♂♀

Rooftop—after school

"And that's why you came to me."

Aoba Kuronuma was leaning back against the railing enclosing the rooftop.

The pair was opposite the rooftop garden—a little relaxation spot for students at the school.

Thanks to the solar panels that powered part of the building, no other students were visible from this location. You would only see the cool and off-kilter types back here.

Raira Academy had almost no "proper" delinquents, which is why the students were allowed access to the roof, but here among the solar panels, there was a different kind of tension than elsewhere on campus.

"Yes. I thought maybe you would know something about that," Yahiro said, somewhat intimidated but remaining cool.

"He shouldn't have made up that stuff about the Headless Rider's favorite treat being castella cake bites. Those are *my* favorite," Aoba said cheerily. "Anyway, I wish I knew where he is, too. I called him as soon as I saw that article."

"Did he answer the phone?"

"No, it was already off by the time I called. Or he was out of network…" He paused, then grinned menacingly. "Or he was *taken* out of network…"

"!"

"What do they say? The people chasing the Headless Rider get abducted by the Headless Rider…?"

"You're saying that Miss Rider abducted him?" Yahiro repeated, feeling nervous.

Aoba's eyes narrowed instantly. "Oh…? 'Miss Rider,' is it…?"

"Ah…"

"So did you meet her with Kuon, then? You met the rider?"

" "

Yahiro didn't say anything. He wasn't sure what was safe to say. But his reaction might as well have been a confirmation.

"You're a bad liar, aren't you?"

"Am I?"

"Aren't you?" Aoba smirked, seemingly enjoying Yahiro's confusion. "To be honest, I don't care if you've met her or not. There's one piece of information I can say to you for certain."

"What's that?"

"The Headless Rider's not the kind of person who goes around abducting others... I mean, she's not a person at all...but that's just making things complicated."

"?"

Yahiro was even more confused. It sounded as though Aoba had known her for years.

"You like tilting your head when you're confused, don't you?"

"Oh, sorry. There's still so much about Tokyo I don't understand..."

"This isn't a Tokyo thing... Anyway, you don't need to think of the Headless Rider as the potential culprit. If she *were* abducting people for some reason, she wouldn't hurt them, in my opinion," Aoba said, smiling self-deprecatingly. "It's simple. The only thing you need to know is...the Headless Rider's just too *nice*."

"Nice?"

"More than any human being. She might be driving without a license, but if she sees someone in trouble, there's a much higher chance that she'll reach out to help than any regular person would, in my opinion."

"Do you know the Headless Rider, then?" Yahiro asked matter-of-factly.

"If I do, we're not close enough friends that I'd tell you," Aoba said. "Right?"

Yahiro thought this over and bowed his head. "I guess you're right. Thank you."

"Huh. So you do understand," Aoba remarked, a little surprised. But as the younger student turned away to leave, he called out to hold him back. "Oh, one more thing."

"?"

"Do you know where to find Kuon's house?"

♂♀

Evening—Takadanobaba

"So this…is Kuon's place…"

Yahiro looked up at the structure before him.

After Aoba told him the location, Yahiro decided to pay a visit to the apartment building with Himeka after school. He was hoping his friend was just sick with a simple cold, but he couldn't eliminate his concern.

The building was quite a long distance from Takadanobaba Station and considerably taller than any other structures nearby. If you stood on the roof, you could see the entire neighborhood around you.

It was over thirty years old, and it didn't have any gate security outside or even a camera at the entrance, by the looks of it.

Himeka gave her honest summation. "It's big but really old."

"It is?" Yahiro replied.

He came from a village where there were no apartment buildings, so he had a different baseline for determining whether a building was new or old. He couldn't see any cracks in the walls, so even in comparison to their school, it didn't seem all that old to him.

"Yes…if a place this big was built recently, you wouldn't be able to get to the individual doors," Himeka said, proceeding into the building.

There was no security at the front or a desk for holding packages. Deliveries would have to go directly to the apartments themselves.

As they rode upward on the elevator, they discussed what to do when they reached Kuon's door.

"What should we tell his family?"

"That he didn't come to school, so we're here to give back a book. That should work," said Himeka, pulling one out of her bag. It was just a book she'd been reading in between classes at school. The title was *Ikebukuro Strikes Back.*

"What book is that?"

"It's a guide to Ikebukuro. The author is named Shinichi Tsukumoya, and it even has a section about the Headless Rider."

"Ohhh…"

He'd done a bit of research about the rider while he was in Akita but only online. He hadn't thought to look up actual books.

I'll need to borrow it later or buy a copy for myself, he thought, right as the elevator reached its destination.

Nozomi & Kuon Kotonami

The nameplate next to the apartment door told them who lived there.

"Is Nozomi…his mom?"

Nozomi was a feminine name, after all. That would suggest that Kuon probably lived with his mother.

Yahiro went ahead and rang the bell. They waited for a while, but no one answered.

"…Maybe nobody's home," Himeka said.

"Should we leave?" Yahiro asked and made to turn around—but then he paused, and he stared at the door itself.

"What's wrong?"

"Someone's inside," he said.

"Huh?"

Yahiro leaned in so that his face was close to the door and spoke loud enough that it could carry inside.

"Excuse me, my name is Mizuchi, and I'm a classmate of Kuon's," he said with a light knock on the door. There was no answer.

"Are you sure you're not imagining things?" Himeka asked.

"No, I heard footsteps."

Yahiro's particular blend of cowardice and the unfathomable accumulation of past experiences that gave rise to it granted him senses that were more sensitive and attuned than most. His sensitivity had been dulled due to the crowds and stimulation of Tokyo, but now that he was getting used to life here, his old touch was coming back.

He could sense delinquents sneaking up on him, carrying their weapons—or people holding their breath to hide from him. These sensations came from tiny sounds in the environment, which Yahiro honed his senses to catch.

The faintest sounds coming from beyond the door told him that someone was still inside.

"What should we do…? I know there's someone in there…but why aren't they responding?"

"What if it's a burglar?"

"…I suppose that could be."

At worst, it could even be an abductor waiting to capture the two of them. Yahiro started to panic, envisioning Kuon collapsed and dying on the floor inside.

"Let's call for the landlord and have them open it."

"…I don't think they're going to do anything that drastic just because you heard footsteps inside," said Himeka, ever the calm and rational one. She examined the area around the doorknob, then exhaled and said to Yahiro, "I think I can handle this type."

"Type of what?"

"Keep an eye out."

"Huh?"

Keep an eye out for what?

But before he could so much as ask, Himeka removed two narrow pieces of metal from her bag, stuck them into the lock, and started swiveling them around.

"Wh-what?!" Yahiro's face went pale as he realized what Himeka was doing. "Um…Tatsugami?!"

"It's open."

"W-wait…what?!" He gaped, feeling an ugly sweat break out on his face.

Himeka reached out with a slender hand, no worries whatsoever, and grabbed the knob.

"…I'm going to open it."

"…O-okay."

Yahiro decided that he could ask her more about this later. He faced the door with nerves humming. Himeka turned the knob and opened the door.

And…

…nobody stood in the doorway.

"…Huh?"

Was he just mistaken? That was Yahiro's first instinct. But then he caught sight of something wriggling and squirming, squatting in the hallway.

" "
...

Technically, the "squirming" was of a figure trembling behind a decorative plant.

"Um, excuse us. We're Kuon's friends," Yahiro said when he realized that the figure was a woman. "Are you his mother?"

The shaking figure slowly peered out from behind the plant, thick glasses on her face, and looked up at him. "D-do I look…that old to you?"

She had a generally gloomy air. The woman put a hand against the wall to get to her feet and stared at Yahiro and Himeka with undisguised wariness.

"The…the l-lock… How did you…?"

"I just rattled the doorknob a few times, and it opened for whatever reason. Maybe your lock is broken," Himeka lied shamelessly. Yahiro stared at Himeka, wide-eyed, but she merely continued, "I'm sorry for startling you like that. Are you Kotonami's family?"

The frightened woman replied, "I'm N-Nozomi Kotonami.

"I'm K-Kuon's…sister."

♂♀

A few minutes later, Yahiro and Himeka had been shown through to the living room and served some tea. They shot each other occasional glances in search of what to talk about first.

But their conversation partner was busy pouring tea from an odd sitting position on the floor, and it was difficult to know when was appropriate to speak and where to start.

Without meeting their eyes, Nozomi Kotonami began to speak.

"Yahiro Mizuchi and Himeka Tatsugami, correct?"

"!"

Earlier he had only introduced himself as Mizuchi, so he was startled to realize she knew his full name.

Himeka asked flatly, "How do you know our names?"

"Of course I know the names of my dear brother's friends," Nozomi said. She giggled, but she strictly avoided eye contact. Something about this struck Yahiro as eerie, but he shrugged it off, telling himself that this was probably some Tokyo thing.

"Um, the thing is, Kuon wasn't at school today," he explained.

"Yes, I know."

"Huh? Then there *was* a reason he didn't show up."

"Yes. There is a reason," she said, wearing a dark and dreary smile. With what seemed like a happy tone, she explained, "He seems to have been *kidnapped by someone* last night, that's why."

"…?"

"He was taken. Abducted. My sweet Kuon."

"Oh no…," Yahiro muttered.

She sounded so casual that he'd assumed she was joking at first, but then he recalled their initial interaction and came to a startling realization.

"Th-then is that why you didn't answer the doorbell earlier? You thought we were the abductors again?"

"No? I was just scared. I get really shy. I can't open the door for anyone but Kuon and delivery people."

"???"

Yahiro was completely at a loss. He looked to Himeka, who was still calm and collected.

"…It doesn't seem like you contacted the police," she observed.

"You're right, I haven't. It would cause trouble for Kuon, and I don't want police in our home for any reason." Nozomi rocked back and forth. She was trembling. "To be honest, this is really hard on me just having you two inside on our first meeting. I hate to insist for my own personal reasons, and after you came all this way, but…"

Her eyes wandered in empty space, and she produced a memo pad and pencil out of nowhere, sliding them across the table.

"C-can you write your cell number down there? Either one of you."

"?"

So she wants our contact information, so we can leave? I guess I can't blame her, since we essentially invaded her home, Yahiro decided. He sent a look toward Himeka and wrote down his phone number on the pad.

"Th-thank you. Drink your tea. I've got some snacks in the fridge, too, so eat something, please."

"Um, okay?" said Yahiro, confused that he wasn't being told to leave.

Nozomi practically crawled out of the room, then made her way to her bedroom at the end of the hallway.

"What was that about? What are we supposed to do?"

"Dunno…"

The two stared at each other, and then Yahiro's phone started ringing.

"Huh?"

It was from an unfamiliar number, which he viewed with suspicion. Yahiro put the phone to his ear.

"Hey! Hi, how are you? Sorry about that! I'm not a very good host!" came the voice of the woman who had just left the living room. *"Whew, I can finally talk normally! Listen, I'm, like,* incredibly *bad at looking other people in the eyes! I get so nervous I can't have a proper conversation! Sorry about that, okay? It has nothing to do with you two! In fact, I like you! I* love *you both!"*

But although her voice was the same, it was so bright and excitable that it sounded like it had to be coming from a different person entirely.

"Um…is that you, Nozomi?"

"Yeah, why? Oh, do you know how to put it on speaker? That way Himeka can talk, too."

"Sorry, I don't."

She guided him through the steps over the phone, and Yahiro managed to activate the unfamiliar function.

"Hellooo? Can you hear me now, Himeka?"

"Yes, I can hear you."

"Okay, great! And I can hear you!"

The phone was now outputting like a stereo speaker, making it possible for them to hold a normal three-person conversation. Yahiro was relieved, although he couldn't necessarily say for sure if this counted as a "normal" conversation—their partner was talking to them from just behind the wall.

"Allow me to properly introduce myself this time! I'm Nozomi Kotonami! I know I seem like a shut-in, but I'm not a total loser—I do provide for myself! And I'm the one paying for Kuon's tuition and living costs."

"Are you a writer or something?" Himeka asked, the first job she could think of that somebody could do without ever leaving home.

"Oh no, not at all!" Nozomi insisted. *"But I guess, in the sense that I use a pen name and write stuff for money, I'm not that far off?"*

"Pen name?"

"Yeah. You could call it a username, too, but since I'm writing articles, pen name *seems like the proper term!"*

From the other end of the call came the name in question.

"Have you ever heard of...Rira Tailtooth Zaiya?"

Rira Tailtooth Zaiya.

It was an outlandish name; it gave no room for assumption of the writer's nationality. Nonetheless, Yahiro realized he recognized it.

Huh? I feel like I saw that name just today...

But before he could pinpoint the exact place in his memory, Himeka said, "You're the administrator of *IkeNew!*, aren't you?"

"Ding-ding-ding! Correct!"

"Ah!" Yahiro murmured as it came to him.

It was the news site that his classmates showed him today, where they had the picture of Kuon with the Headless Rider. The name of that blog was *IkeNew!*, and the administrator was named Rira Tailtooth Zaiya.

"Huh? But then..."

"That's right. Me and my brother cooked up that article! You'll never find the 'original blog' it came from. I made up that article based on a fictional blog that never existed! It's funny how badly it fooled everyone!"

"? ? ?"

Question marks appeared and vanished in sequence over Yahiro's head.

Making an article based on a fake journal?

What's the point of that?

And why slip in those lies about the Headless Rider?

Should a news website really be making things up?

Then who abducted Kuon?

As the questions rushed through Yahiro's mind, Himeka leaned over the phone to ask, "Did you write that...so that someone would abduct him?"

"...What's this? How sharp of you."

"..."

"So what are you suggesting, Miss Tatsugami? That you have a hunch who did it?" Nozomi's question was a strange one.

Yahiro pushed the doubts out of his mind and said, "That can't be right."

"Why not?"

"Because if you knew who's responsible, you could just tell the police."

"I didn't think that I would hear such a straightforward, innocent opinion in this conversation!" The woman on the other end chuckled. Yahiro couldn't tell what was so funny about that. *"Yahiro, you're funnier than I thought. Just out of curiosity, who do* you *suppose kidnapped everyone?"*

Yahiro considered this carefully and offered, "Maybe an organized criminal group…"

"Why do you think that?"

"I don't know if it's proof, but…I was abducted in the second year of middle school."

"…"

"…"

Himeka and Nozomi said nothing. Both of them understood that Yahiro was not the kind of person who would joke about that sort of thing. But without knowing *why* he was kidnapped, they couldn't say anything. Himeka had no idea what he was talking about, and Nozomi, who'd heard the rumors about Yahiro, hadn't expected such a thing to have happened to him.

"My grandma cleared things up with someone important from the gang to set me free, but it was really scary when it happened."

"You're fascinating, you know that?" Nozomi said, her voice quieter. *"Uh-huh. No wonder Kuon likes you."*

"Um, so is Kuon all right?" Yahiro asked bluntly. "You don't seem that panicked about him to me."

The victim's sister said blithely, *"Well, I don't know if he's 'all right,' but I bet he's got a plan to win.*

"Like your princess over there guessed…he got himself abducted on purpose."

CHAPTER 6 B
The Observers

Tokyo

Going back to half a day earlier—late at night, after Yahiro and Celty met on the street...

The blindfold came off Shiki's eyes, and he was in an unfamiliar room.

Based on the tools present, from the stacks of cardboard boxes in the corner, the kerosene containers, and the trowels hung up on the wall, this was probably some kind of storage room at a mansion.

There wasn't a single window, which made it likely to be a basement, too. With that in mind, he looked toward the person who took the blindfold off.

Shiki's hands were tied up with tape behind his back, and his feet were bound the same way. He was helpless to do anything but look and speak, but he didn't raise a fuss. He focused on the situation, calmly and rationally.

Who was the fool with a death wish who abducted them and brought them here?

The disguise was sunglasses, a face mask, and a hat—the kind of incognito wear that actually drew attention among the public. He wanted to tell them to stick to wearing ski masks but chose to keep his silence for now.

So it wasn't Shiki who spoke first but another man who was on the ground at his feet.

"What the hell do you people want?! You think you're gonna get away with this?!"

It was a man with a shaved head who typically drove the car for Shiki.

"Don't make a fuss," Shiki warned. His underling flinched and glanced up at Shiki. His limbs were also bound, but he had been tossed onto the floor rather than seated in a chair like his boss.

"M...Mr. Shiki! I'm so sorry! It's my fault... It's my fault I let this happen to you!"

"Stop screaming. And my title is director," Shiki warned his panicking companion.

He reflected on what events had led to this situation.

Damn, this is a pain in the ass. What the hell are they after?

One hour earlier, he was out in Tokyo, having finished up a meeting with a business partner. Shiki got into his vehicle so that he and his driver could return to the Awakusu-kai office and report the results of that meeting.

When he didn't hear the usual, "Welcome back, sir," from the driver, Shiki's brain instantly shifted into emergency mode.

Calmly, he looked into the rear mirror like he always did. The man in the driver's seat was bald, like the driver, but it was clear from a glance that he was not the same man who'd driven him to this parking garage.

Shiki was a yakuza, but because their group wasn't in an all-out war right now, he wasn't packing any pistols or blades. Under the current law, possession of a single illegal weapon could expose the head of the entire organization to legal peril.

The question is, is this a personal vendetta against me, or is it an attack on the Awakusu-kai? That makes a big difference. It could be the Asuki-gumi, who still haven't made peace with us, or one of the other groups we're squabbling with… Or maybe it's someone within our organization… I hate that I can't rule that out.

He checked the side doors, to see if he could still get out, but saw that escaping was a fool's errand now. Menacing men wearing sunglasses and masks approached both sides of the car and opened the doors.

The men addressed him brusquely.

"Mr. Shiki?"

"You're coming with us."

Shiki's eyebrows rose. The instant he saw the way they comported themselves, he felt keenly that something was off. It was something he could only have felt because of his years of experience in the underworld society—but he didn't want to believe that his instinct was correct in this circumstance.

"…You want me?" he asked softly.

"I can't answer that question."

"What happened to my driver?"

"If you cooperate with us, we won't harm either of you," said the man, his voice muffled by the mask. Shiki's eyes narrowed, and he examined not the suspicious individuals around him but the inside of the car.

These men did not appear to have guns or any weapons of the sort. If they had concealed weapons, they weren't holding them, which meant they were confident they could handle anything that happened.

But when he noticed there were at least a dozen more people outside the windows, all covering their faces, Shiki let out a little sigh.

Dammit. Akabayashi or Aozaki would probably be able to handle this many of them. But I'm not the combat-first type. This is what I get for that, I suppose.

"Don't cause trouble, and we won't kill you. You have my word."

…What the…?

Shiki sensed a particular emotion disguised behind the man's tone of voice.

"All right," he snapped coldly. "Let's hear you out."

He'd been loaded into a van they had parked nearby, then blindfolded and driven around for about an hour before reaching a destination.

Based on the movement of the car, he could tell that they hadn't tried to confuse him by going on and off the highway or turning in circles to throw off his sense of direction. Given the length of time he'd spent in the moving vehicle and the nature of this storage room, he guessed it was likely to be a mansion on the western edge of the Tokyo metropolitan area, somewhere like Fuchu or Hachioji.

No, I shouldn't make any assumptions, Shiki told himself.

To the men in the basement with him, he asked, "So what do you want with me?"

"Nothing, apparently."

"What?"

"If anything, it's just to have you stay here for a while, I guess."

Ah. So I won't get anywhere with these ones. They must be bottom-rung muscle who don't know any details. Actually, if my guess is right, they're not on any *rung at all...*

There was an outburst of noise from the entrance, interrupting his thoughts.

The door opened, and another group of men piled into the room. In the gaps past them, Shiki could see a staircase leading upward. So it *was* a basement.

Shiki turned his attention to the newcomers. Of the three who had just arrived, two of them had their faces covered with masks, like the others.

The last of the three was a boy tied up like Shiki and his driver, and there was no missing the bright green hair on his head.

"Stay in here and shut up."

"I'd prefer to be in a room with a pretty lady, if possible," the boy said. The men ignored him and shoved him forward.

As he toppled forward near Shiki's feet, the boy shouted loud enough for everyone to hear, "I know they're here! I know Aya and Ai Tatsugami are in this building somewhere!"

One of the men slowly and menacingly pressed his foot against the boy's stomach.

"Shut up."

"Ow, ow, ow! I give up! I yield! I'll be quiet, just stop—please!"

The men gave the boy chilling glares and left without even removing his blindfold. There was one of them left as a guard at the door, but he had no intention of talking to any of them. He just leaned against the wall without a word.

Judging that it was safe for them to talk, however, Shiki spoke to the boy at his feet. "You all right, kid?"

"Oh, thanks. Could you at least get my blindfold off?"

"Sorry, I'm not one of them. I'm not blindfolded, but my hands and feet are tied up, just like yours."

"Oh, I gotcha. Sorry about that."

Shiki gave the boy an appraising look, then murmured under his breath, "You're the one everyone was talking about online this morning."

"Huh? You know me, too, mister?"

"It wasn't a site I usually browse, but I was doing a little research into the Headless Rider, see."

"Aw, geez. So I'm famous now?" The boy laughed awkwardly.

"Yeah," Shiki said. "And I know you're a liar, too."

"Huh?"

"The Headless Rider doesn't have a favorite food. The Headless Rider doesn't eat at all. And why would she go out to karaoke? She doesn't have a head."

"Gee, mister, you actually believe the Headless Rider is some monster without a head?" the boy mocked.

Shiki countered with simple facts. "I don't have to believe. What doesn't exist doesn't exist. If you've met Celty in person, you should know better than anyone."

"...Calm down, mister. With the way you're acting and the fact that you know the Headless Rider's name...are you *in the business*?" the boy joked.

Shiki's subordinate, who was tied up at his feet, snarled, "Who the fuck do you think you are, talkin' to the boss like that? Huh?"

Shiki sighed at the outburst and ignored his driver to speak to the boy again, but he couldn't get the words out first.

"Director," said his henchman, "I know this kid. He's the one the guys at the office were yellin' about." His voice was agitated; he had recognized the green hair.

"He's the friend of the kid who was goin' at it with Shizuo Heiwajima."

♂♀

Ikebukuro West Gate Park—daytime

At the outdoor stage area in West Gate Park, there was an odd combination of figures sitting on a metal tube bench: a man in a bartender's outfit and a woman in a black riding suit.

"So that Yahiro boy really fought evenly against you, Shizuo?" Celty typed, then showed off the screen of the smartphone. The man in the bartender uniform, Shizuo Heiwajima, didn't bother to evade the question.

"Yeah, he was with the green-haired kid, right? Then that's him, all right."

He looked up at the sky, seeming to reminisce on the event, even though it was only a few days ago.

"I had no idea you knew him, Celty. Small world."

"No, I only met him yesterday... So much has happened, I can barely keep track of it."

Upon hearing that Shiki had gone missing, Celty had taken it upon herself to do some independent investigation around the city. Akabayashi warned her that some folks suspected her of being guilty, and she was at a loss for what to do next when Shizuo spotted her and said hi.

Celty recalled the conversation between Yahiro and Libei last night and decided to bring it up as a long shot. She was stunned when he actually confirmed it.

"I can't believe it. I might believe if it was Simon, but a normal teenager being able to hang in your presence? It's stunning."

"Uh, what do you think I am, exactly?"

"Sorry. It's just that I've never seen you struggle in a normal fistfight."

In Celty's head, she was envisioning a certain info dealer, but that was anything but a "normal fistfight," and she didn't want to upset Shizuo, so she chose not to mention him.

Strangely enough, however, Shizuo brought up the topic all on his own.

"You remember Izaya?"

"How could I not…? I'm surprised you mentioned his name, actually."

"Well, it's not like I want to remember that fleabrain… Anyway, I hate to even ask you for this favor, but if you know that Yahiro Mizuchi kid, could you just keep an eye on him for me?"

"?"

She tilted her helmet to the side to indicate puzzlement. Shizuo made a conflicted face and said, "That guy with the green dyed hair… he's the same type of person as that Izaya asshole."

"Is that right?"

"Just a hunch."

"I see."

Yes, the friendly way he tried to sidle up to me was clearly unnatural, Celty thought, recalling when he had approached her for the photo.

She'd seen it show up in the news this morning. The story was embellished with nonsense about castella cake bites and karaoke, but the important thing to Celty was that it had a strong "not the kidnapper" vibe to it, so she was more relieved than angry about it.

"But how does that tie in to being concerned about Yahiro? If this guy's really like Izaya, then he's going to drag everyone around him into disaster," Celty typed out.

Shizuo thought it over and replied, "I dunno. Fighting with that kid kind of reminded me of my old self."

"Your old self?"

"When you're as strong as him, you find yourself getting dragged into all kinds of crap. I've never seen him around the city before. Maybe he got in trouble somewhere else and came here to get away from it," Shizuo said and thought some more. He clicked his tongue. "Hey, Celty."

"What?"

"I'm just spitballing here. What if everything went right for me… and I got along properly with Izaya, like I do with Shinra. What do you think would've happened?"

"That's quite a question," Celty said, not hiding her shock. *"But why would you ask me that?"*

"I dunno…that building that got busted up a year and a half ago—they finally finished it in the last six months…"

"Oh, that one."

A year and a half ago, Shizuo had been caught in an incident and had fought a true battle to the death with his nemesis, Izaya Orihara.

Izaya had vanished from the city, so nobody knew if he was alive or dead, but the scars of their tremendous battle remained on the town for a while. The explosion at the partially built building was especially bad, but because the culprit who caused it was gone, there hadn't been any progress in bringing him to justice.

They probably suspected that Shizuo had something to do with it, but the fact that he hadn't even been brought in for questioning meant they were either letting him swim, or there was some kind of special activity going on within the police department.

The explosion delayed the building's construction significantly, but Celty remembered that it was very nearly complete around the time she left on her vacation with Shinra.

"I was remembering what happened with that building...and not that I *wanted* to envision it, but I wondered, if I was actually friends with that fleabrain, would it have saved the city a whole lot of grief...?"

I think...

She was going to type *That's not true* but stopped. Yes, considering that some people were victims of Shizuo and Izaya's fighting, it was tempting to imagine that everyone could have lived peacefully if not for their rivalry.

Celty would have been one of them.

"Well, that might be true, but it also could've been much worse."

"You think so?"

"Yes. It wouldn't mean that Izaya would be a saint, for one thing. If you were friends, he could have just used you and gotten you to ruin all kinds of things."

"Yeah...that makes sense." Shizuo exhaled, then said to his friend, "This Yahiro guy, while we were locked in our fight, it was like...I dunno...like he was happy. I feel like every time up until then, he was fighting against his will."

"Are there fights that aren't against your will?"

"Dunno. For me, when I was up against those people controlled by that sword, and I could use my strength for real for the first time in my life...I dunno. It was fun," Shizuo said simply and looked away. He seemed to be embarrassed by what he had said. "I don't know—I think maybe he felt the same way I did back then… Like, if he's that strong, he's gonna have all kinds of people coming up to him. If that fleabrain was still around, he'd definitely have gotten in touch with him."

"I get that."

"So part of it is that he's from my old school…but it's best if nobody else goes through what me and that fleabrain did. But also, I can't just let him get manipulated by someone who's just like the fleabrain… Of course, he's his own person, so I shouldn't get into his business. If anything happens, could you just tell him not to turn out like me? For his own sake?"

"You could tell him yourself," Celty said, but that just brought a furrow to Shizuo's brow.

"You or Shinra or Tom could talk to him. But if I'm the one reaching out to a normal high schooler, he's gonna end up having to deal with a bunch of other bullshit."

I don't know…, Celty thought. *In that vein, if Yahiro is getting along with the Headless Rider, then I'm inflicting the same thing on him as Shizuo. Speaking of which…if he'll talk to me, does that mean he doesn't mind making* me *deal with a bunch of other bullshit?*

She wanted to bring that up and rub his face in it but decided that it wasn't really fair. He was just trying to be considerate of the kid.

He's really relaxed a lot if he's having thoughts like this, though. But I guess I understand why he's not on edge anymore, with Izaya out of the picture.

Celty welcomed this change in her friend. She got up from the bench and said, *"Sorry for interrupting your break time. I should be going."*

"You sure? Seems like you've got headaches of your own. Anything I can help you with?"

"No, I'm fine."

If he was calmer these days, she couldn't go dragging him back into trouble. Celty was more concerned with her friend's future. She'd have to look elsewhere for clues to Shiki's whereabouts…

"Miss Headless Rider!"

There was a voice calling for her.

Shizuo and Celty turned in the direction of the sound and saw a girl. She was out of breath, having run to catch up, and once she could speak again, she put on a dazzling smile.

"Finally... I finally found you!"

Huh? Wait a moment...

Before she could remember the name of the familiar girl, Shizuo said the answer.

"Oh, hey, Akane."

Ah, yes, that's right. Akane.

Akane Awakusu.

The granddaughter of Dougen Awakusu, the feared leader of the Awakusu-kai. A few years ago, she had come into close contact with Celty and Shizuo in a string of dangerous events.

"Sh-Shizuo! Hello," she said, flustered, bowing to him. Then she turned back to Celty. "I'm so glad you've come back!"

"Yes, I know I was away on a vacation for quite a while..."

"Vacation?"

"Yes. We spent half a year traveling all over, from fireworks festivals in Akita down to the Kerama Islands in Okinawa."

She didn't have much interaction with Akane outside of the incident in question, so why would she be so enthusiastic and delighted about her return to Ikebukuro? But Celty ignored this question and gave her a straightforward answer.

Akane looked utterly relieved. In fact, she nearly had tears in her eyes.

"I'm glad...I'm so glad that you weren't the culprit."

"Oh, about that?"

"Yes... As a matter of fact, a girl from my school went missing...and she was a huge fan of yours!"

What? Celty froze.

Shizuo frowned and muttered, "A...fan of Celty's?"

Once she heard the details, a number of things fell into place for Celty. *I see now. Yesterday, Yahiro mentioned that a younger kid he knew was searching for her upperclassman... How surprising that she turned out to be Akane.*

It was a very strange place for a connection like that to pop up. Celty marveled at the twists and turns of fate or perhaps the fact that the world was a smaller place than she realized.

Then she remembered that there were more important things at the moment and thumped her chest to set Akane at ease.

"Don't worry. I'm going to make sure that I find your friend and Mr. Shiki."

But to her surprise, Akane immediately looked worried. "Huh?"

"Huh?"

"What do you mean…and Mr. Shiki?"

Oh, shoot!

Apparently, Akane didn't know yet that Shiki had been missing since last night. Shizuo wasn't aware of the facts, either, but he could tell that Celty had said something she shouldn't have. He gave her a very painful glance that said, *What are you doing?*

"No, it's not like that. I made a typo. I was trying to say, I'll find your friend with Mr. Shiki. Stupid typo."

"You're lying, aren't you?"

Her attempt at a quick cover-up was woefully unconvincing.

"…I'm sorry. I thought you knew already."

After that, Akane insisted that she wanted to search for the real kidnapper, too, but Celty managed to talk her out of it and learned everything she could offer in terms of information. What really worried her was what she said next.

"Miss Tatsugami said…you were like a god to her."

"A god."

"I'm not exaggerating… She said you would change her world…and that if she could be like you, she would be happy to die…"

"This girl has some violent ideas."

Then again, there was that other girl who got plastic surgery to look like me, Celty recalled, thinking of the girl who was supposedly now living in America. *Mr. Shiki said something about a person who disappeared while searching for me. It feels weird to hear the word* fan, *but when I hear someone treats me like a god, I just feel sorry for them. I'm not that special.*

"Anyway," Celty typed, *"leave the rest up to people like me and Mr. Akabayashi. Please don't do anything dangerous, Akane."*

Celty would feel horrible if something bad happened to Akane for associating with her, plus she didn't know how the Awakusu-kai might react to that. So she made sure to stress that Akane was not to go off looking for the culprit alone.

"But that's what Mr. Shiki said, too..."

"*It's all right! Just trust me! I know I was gone for half a year, but I came back, didn't I?*" Celty insisted, trying to force the discussion to a close. Her vehemence won out, and Akane reluctantly accepted her argument.

"*Just sit tight and wait. I'll bring back your friend from school and Mr. Shiki too,*" Celty typed, making the font larger.

Shizuo added, "Hey, I'll help, too. Is there anything I can do?"

"*If it turns into something bigger and messier than I can handle, I'll ask you for help. Until then...you could ask and see if Tom or whoever knows anything about this.*"

"Sure thing. Call me whenever. I'll skip work to help out," Shizuo said with a reassuring chuckle.

As she left, Celty thought, *If it's something that I need Shizuo's help to solve, it's going to have to be a whole pack of vampires or something...*

If Shizuo went straight into rage mode, he could wipe out just about any criminal element. But in this case, there were victims to rescue. If he got violent, it could spell danger for the hostages, and freeing them was the top priority here.

Celty got onto the black motorcycle she kept parked at the entrance to the park. It was all she could do to pray that the kidnapped people were still alive enough to count as hostages.

Just then, she felt an unpleasant sensation on her spine and spun around.

She saw Akane and Shizuo looking her way and waving, so in the process of turning, she used her unearthly sense of vision to peer all over the park.

What is it? I could swear I sensed someone watching. Something different than the usual curious stare...

Then she reached the possibility that it could have been the traffic cop, felt her skin crawl, and decided to leave.

The very person who was gazing at the Headless Rider waited for the motorcycle to vanish before murmuring, "Shizuo Heiwajima is fine. But not the girl."

She was in a car parked next to West Gate Park, watching Shizuo and Akane through narrowed eyes.

"She's got to go," the woman said. Her voice took on an unfathomable longing similar to love. "She's too involved. The Great One is going to make her disappear."

There was nothing but hatred and pity for Akane Awakusu in her eyes. The smile plastered on her face was like that of a broken puppet whose soul had left its body.

"That's simply her fate."

♂♀

Basement garage of Shinra's apartment building—evening

"Here we are again, one day later."

Celty Sturluson had raced all over town collecting information and returned to the basement parking lot. When she got off her motorcycle, she was greeted by the young man she'd met for the first time just last night.

…?!

…Oh, it's Libei Ying.

She was relieved that it was someone she actually knew—if only since last night, when they traded information—but then realized something alarming and whipped out her smartphone.

"How did you know I'd be here?! I gave you my e-mail address, not my address-address!"

"What can I say? Once a scoundrel, always a scoundrel… You don't need to worry, though. I'm not going to turn you over to the cops or the media." Libei grinned innocently.

Celty thought his response over and noticed something. *"Oh, right... The Dragon Zombies were aligned with Izaya for a while. You must have heard from him back then, right?"*

"Well, I've never met the info broker named Izaya Orihara in person. When I was hospitalized, some of my friends used his services. But how can I thank him for that now, when I don't know if he's alive or dead?"

"Good question. He's just proved that he can be a royal pain in the ass to me, alive or dead," Celty said with a shrug.

Libei repeated the gesture. "Heroes and villains are labels created by others. In the last six months, while your life or death could not be ascertained, they turned *you* into a villain, didn't they?"

"You didn't come here just to trade barbs with me, did you?"

"No, and I thank you for being right to the point. Something happened with the Awakusu-kai, didn't it?"

"What are you talking about?" Celty asked him carefully, considering that he might be bluffing to lure info out of her.

"The guys in Jan-Jaka-Jan were bein' a real pain in the ass about it this morning. Apparently, they suspect us of something?"

Jan-Jaka-Jan was a rival gang to Dragon Zombie, and they enjoyed the protection and affiliation of the Awakusu-kai. They had to be, assuming that only a group with considerable power would dare do something as brazen as abducting a lieutenant of the Awakusu-kai.

But it was hard to imagine Dragon Zombie going above their rival motorcycle gang to mess with their yakuza backers instead. In that sense, Celty had tentatively removed Libei from her list of suspects.

"We don't want to be under suspicion, you understand. So I'm willing to put my full resources into helping you."

"What? Are you going to tell me who the busiest street gangs are nowadays?"

If some kind of criminal enterprise was behind this, and they captured Shiki, knowing that he was a principal member of the Awakusu-kai, that would mean they had the strength to act with hostility toward the yakuza.

So Celty asked that question, assuming there could be some other yakuza syndicate involved. But Libei just shook his head.

"Just the opposite. There are people—and groups—who completely vanished from Ikebukuro altogether."

Celty considered this skeptically and typed, *"You're not saying...
Izaya Orihara is controlling things from the shadows, are you?"*

"No, no, I'm not saying that. It's just that you can't eliminate the
possibility. At the very least, I'm talking about a group Izaya Orihara
was involved with. Both of them, actually."

"...Both?"

"That's right. There are two of them. I'd guess you already know
them, don't you?" Libei said, twirling around like a tease. He leaned
back against a pillar and said, "I'm talking about Amphisbaena, the
underground gambling group, and Heaven's Slave, the drug dealers."

"Oh... That's right, they're..."

Celty had heard those names before. They were groups that Izaya
Orihara destroyed.

She only learned the details long after it happened, but when Izaya
was eliminating them both together, he had utilized her to run an
errand for him.

"They didn't just vanish. They were eliminated."

"But the roots are still alive."

"Is that a fact?"

"Yes, it is. The central person in each group is still alive and around.
Izaya Orihara was the one holding the reins for them, but now he's
gone, isn't he? So each group temporarily became active again."

Libei was talking easily and casually, but there was no denying a bit
of an edge lurking beneath his voice. Celty took that to mean these
groups were hostile to the Dragon Zombies when they were around.

*"And you're saying they vanished recently? They weren't just crushed
by the Awakusu-kai?"*

"In that case, I would at least have heard a whiff of a rumor about
it. But they're simply gone, like smoke evaporating into the air... Like
they sank from the underworld of the city to somewhere even lower."

"Do they really have something to do with this?"

He was making it sound eerie, but that alone didn't mean they were
involved in the abductions. For one thing, just because Izaya was
using her to run errands when he destroyed the groups didn't mean
they should bear some misguided grudge against Celty.

Then again, Izaya's gone, so maybe they think I was his ally, and they have no one else to turn their hatred upon. *Still, that's not enough of a case to pin the label of "true culprit" on them.*

She typed, *"Do you have any more evidence?"*

"You're sharp. I can't hide anything from you," he teased, shrugging. Then Libei wiped the smile off his face and continued in dead earnest. "About half a year ago, he made contact with us. Wanted us to do a job for him and swore the money had no strings attached. It was a sketchy story and would've antagonized the Awakusu-kai for no good reason, so we turned it down...but then he said something."

Libei paused and stared Celty right in the face.

"...How much can you really trust the Headless Rider?"

"What's that supposed to mean?"

"Just what it sounds like. He was asking if we believed you were some inhuman creature beyond the bounds of human reason. Kept asking, real persistent. I swear it was turning him on or something."

"And who was this guy you're talking about?" Celty prompted.

Libei answered, "The kanji in his name mean 'four hundred thousand'...but you read them 'Shijima.' You know him?"

"...Never heard the name," she typed. But just after she showed him, she had a sudden start and retyped her message. *"No, wait. Shijima, Shijima... Yes, that's him."*

The image that came to Celty's memory was of a young man she observed working as an assistant of sorts to a man named Nasujima a year and a half ago.

He'd seemed like a nondescript, frightened boy at the time, but she remembered that he had that strange last name.

"A little while after I turned him down, he vanished from the city. From what I understand, he was going around asking about you quite a lot," Libei said. He smiled again and continued gleefully, "Then someone started a rumor—a rumor that the Headless Rider made him vanish."

"You don't think..."

"Yep. The very first person to disappear and launch the rumor that he was kidnapped by the Headless Rider. But at that point, it was pretty much only a thing among folks like us. Then, a little while later, the people searching around for the Headless Rider started disappearing. First, it was one. Then two within a month. Five in three months, fifteen in half a year... The pace is increasing."

"I see... So it's worth looking into him." Celty felt emboldened by this valuable piece of information. She told the unexpected visitor, *"Thank you. This might be the breakthrough I need. I'll let the others know."*

"What others, exactly? Like Yahiro Mizuchi?"

"Yeah... I mean, I promised I would tell him if I learned anything."

"It's probably better if you don't involve him in this," Libei said, a rare admonishment.

Celty typed, *"Well, I agree it's better not to drag children into trouble, but I think it would be a good idea just to reassure him that I've got a good clue. If I don't tell him the actual name, he can't go searching, right?"*

"Ahhh, I see. But what I meant was that if you let him know more about this, he's going to get attached to you."

"Attached...?"

"See, we're trying to get him in with us. Ever since the previous head of the group rose to that position, we've been recruiting Japanese people to join the gang, rather than keeping it limited to the Taiwanese." The effeminate young man smirked. Celty couldn't tell how serious he was being and recalled what Shizuo said during the day.

"Are there different groups trying to recruit him now?"

"Oh, sure. It's been all the talk of Ikebukuro the last few days, along with your return. Though I think very few of the gangs have actually learned Yahiro's name so far."

"I understand that he's a powerful fighter...but what specifically do you see in him?" Celty inquired.

Libei grinned gleefully and looked away, "Well, he's a true, authentic monster. I haven't shivered like that in ages."

"Monster, huh?" snorted Celty.

Libei understood exactly what she meant. "Your body might be monstrous. But your heart is more human than human. That's how we can have a friendly conversation like this. But that boy? He might be much less human than you are."

He felt an unpleasant, sticky sweat break out on his back, recalling their fight the evening before.

"I think it's a normal reaction to get more aggressive because you're scared," he said, to cover up his own fear, "but in his case, that reaction has absolutely no hesitation to it whatsoever. He wields that fear like a weapon, the way that others use anger or hatred. You've seen that in manga, right? When someone falls into peril, and instantly their true power manifests and blows the enemy away..."

"*Yes, I'm familiar.*"

"It's like he can unlock that part of his brain with just the smallest touch of fear," Libei said. Wryly, he added, "If I hadn't actually seen Shizuo Heiwajima or the Headless Rider for myself, I would never think of allying myself with you. I'd want to eliminate you as quickly as possible...you see?"

"*You're being too honest for your own good.*"

"Oops, sorry, sorry. But hey, once he actually met you and Shizuo, maybe he felt relieved. Did you notice that? Last night he was wary of you, but all things considered, he actually seemed pretty happy, didn't he?"

"I bet that where he used to live, without Shizuo or you around, he must've had a really hard time."

♂♀

Outside of Himeka's house—Ikebukuro

The first thing she noticed when she tried to open the door was that it wouldn't open.

Locked doors were normal, perhaps, but Himeka wasn't carrying a spare key.

Or to be more specific, she wasn't *allowed* to carry a spare.

The lights were on inside, but there was no response when she rang the doorbell.

It's happened again. The interval's getting shorter, she thought without external signs of concern.

Her mother was probably in a state again inside—she'd been going into these spasmodic episodes periodically ever since Himeka was a very young child.

It was either some illness of the mind, or an act she'd been carrying on with, or some kind of ritual.

She would simply shut out all external stimuli, without warning, and speak directly into the wall.

It was like the world she consciously recognized existed only within her shadow on the wall. Anything she had to say to Himeka, or her sisters, or their father, or anyone else who lived in the neighborhood, had to be spoken directly to her own shadow.

While she was doing this, she reacted to virtually nothing anyone said to her. And if she did, she would still say her answer to the shadow.

You might think she was having some kind of wonderful dream within that shadow, but to listen to the solitary "conversation," it did not sound all that wonderful.

Himeka envisioned her mother pressing her forehead against the wall, gently grating her own skin, having a conversation with some unseen person. She set down her bag.

For the second time today, she removed a special metal tool that looked like a hairpin. It was tempting to think of it as a locksmith's pick, but this was quite different from the professional thing.

Of course, there was no way she could come into possession of real lockpicking tools. Most regular people weren't even allowed to own those lockpicks, unless they were a locksmith with a proper license. Selling them to anyone who didn't possess that qualification was a crime.

She couldn't have locksmith credentials at her age, which would make this action illegal—but there were exceptions if you had a valid reason.

She didn't know if "opening your own door because you regularly got locked out" counted as a valid reason, but to Himeka, it was.

Today, for the very first time, she picked the lock of another person's door. Including today, she had only used her tools and expertise twice on any lock other than her own.

The first time was to save a classmate in middle school who was locked in the school storage room as a prank. If that counted as a crime, so be it.

Opening the door today was out of concern for Kuon, thinking the culprit might still be inside. That probably wouldn't qualify as an excuse, though.

When she lied to Kuon's sister Nozomi, right to her face, then how was she really any different from a burglar? Himeka figured that there wasn't a meaningful distinction there.

In fact, given that she felt absolutely no guilt about doing it, she might be even worse than a burglar. This thought and more ran through her mind as she stuck her lockpicking tool into the front door of her home.

On the way home after talking with Kuon's sister, she assumed that Yahiro was creeped out and disgusted after witnessing her lockpicking in action.

She didn't mind; she'd earned that reaction. If he suspected her of being a regular burglar or started rumors about her, she'd earned that, too.

But Yahiro wasn't creeped out. Instead, he brought up the topic right away in the elevator.

"I was amazed at how quickly you opened that door. Who taught you how to do that?"

"Someone three years older than me when I was in elementary school. They lived in the neighborhood," Himeka said, startled at the question, though she had no reason to hide any of it. "I don't know how *they* knew how to do it, but they taught me after seeing how often I got locked out of the house."

"Locked out of the house?"

"It's a family thing. We didn't get to carry spare keys around, but the door was quite often locked when we got home."

"Wow. That sounds tough," said Yahiro. He went on to explain that his home was a hot springs inn that was open year-round with people coming and going all the time, so someone was always there, and he never really had to think about keys and locks. Maybe he simply accepted her story at face value, thinking that it was common for people who lived in the big city.

She said nothing to that, so Yahiro followed with "Thanks for today."

"Huh?"

"If you weren't with me, I wouldn't have been able to meet Kuon's sister."

"..."

She wasn't going to say anything to that, either, but decided better of it. She sighed and summed him up in one short statement.

"You really are a little strange, Mizuchi."

"I am?"

"Normally, when you see someone doing what I did, you'd think they were a burglar, wouldn't you?"

Yahiro admitted, "Oh yeah. The reason I was startled earlier is because I thought it was what a burglar would do."

He sounded very confident in his answer, as though trying to reinforce that he was normal.

"Then you must be disgusted with me, right?"

"Do you rob houses?"

"No."

"Then there's no reason for me to hate you."

It felt like Kuon would say something like, "What kind of blunt conversation is this?!" if he was present. But Yahiro just reminisced on his past and said, "Oh, and the burglar I know just smashed the lock open with a hammer. When I saw it and yelled at him, he came running to hit *me* with the hammer next. So that was way more shocking than when I saw you do it."

"I wonder if I was supposed to laugh at that..."

She couldn't tell if he had been serious or joking, but either way, it was clear he had been doing his best to cheer her up. So she felt a bit bad that she'd reacted with her usual flat mask.

She cleared the door lock to her home at last.

"I'm home," she said on pure reflex when she saw the figure inside, assuming it was her mother.

But...

"...? ...!"

She realized someone else was there.

Then she sensed multiple figures just outside, behind the door she'd just passed through.

Before she could say a word, she was grabbed and immobilized from behind.

♂♀

"Whoa…whoa, whoa, whoa! What the hell's goin' on over there?!"

On a lot a short distance away from Himeka's house, a number of people had snuck into the yard to watch Himeka, and the event currently unfolding left them stunned.

Out of nowhere, several men rushed up to the doorway of Himeka's house, then grabbed her and started to drag her out to a van waiting just outside.

"Wh-what should we do, Mr. Horada?"

"Do? I mean…what? What's going on?!"

Horada was in a state of utter confusion. He and his followers were on a quest to recruit the kid who could fight against Shizuo, and they were using their younger members to do a little research on the boy.

His name was Yahiro Mizuchi, and he was from Akita. Since the first day of school, he'd been hanging out with the green-haired boy, Kuon Kotonami, and he was friends with another student named Himeka Tatsugami. Horada decided to put his plan into motion by starting with the girl.

"Did someone else have the same idea as us and kidnap her first?" wondered Horada, who had a mind for wicked ideas. He'd considered taking her hostage and forcing Yahiro to do what he said.

But considering that the plan was for a much longer relationship, he decided that rather than using the quickest possible method, he should try to make the boy owe him a favor and pull him in that way.

They had followed Himeka back to her house so that they knew where it was and were just discussing what to do next when the event unfolded before their eyes.

"What should we do? Save her?"

"N-nah, those guys look pretty burly…"

"But I thought you said you kidnapped the Yellow Scarves' leader's girl once."

"Kidnapping and saving are different things, dumbass!" Horada snapped shamefully. He tried to get his panicked mind to focus. "Dammit, what now? If those guys are Awakusu-kai, we can't mess with them, definitely not…"

"What if we go to the cops and explain that we just happened to see it?"

"The cops...? I don't want the cops." Horada grunted, remembering the face of the traffic cop who arrested him. The memory sent a chill through his body. "Ahhh, shit! Think, think, think! C'mon!"

At last, he decided on a method of prolonging the decision.

"Hey, you! Get your motorcycle and follow that car," he ordered.

One of the younger guys helping him trail Himeka came here on a motorcycle, Horada remembered, so he ordered him to go around to the backstreet where it was parked and follow the van.

"Huh? I-I've never followed a car before!"

"If you can follow a person, you can follow a car! Just do it!"

"Y-yes, sir!"

The younger guy rushed off for his bike, giving Horada a moment to think.

There we go. If we follow them and find out that they look weak, then we'll roll in and take 'em out and save the girl, so he'll owe me one. And if they're the Awakusu-kai...then I can pretend I didn't see anything, he decided smoothly.

But just then, he saw a shadow burst out of the doorway of Himeka's house.

"What the—?"

Horada squinted at the figure, who was ordering the men around and heading back to the van.

"A woman...?"

INTERMISSION
Online Rumors (5)

On the Ikebukuro information site IkeNew! Version I.KEBU.KUR.O

New Post: [Sad News]
Green-haired boy who made friends with
headless rider is missing!

A selection of twits from the social network Twittia

I can't get in touch with that guy **** from IkeNew this morning.

→ Seriously?

→ I think he's gone missing. Nobody answers the phone at his house.

→ Missing?

→ Because he learned the Headless Rider's secret?

Comment from IkeNew! *Administrator*

Vanished, he has.

Coming from the Blue Squares, these twits appear to be.

So despite his green hair, blue the young lad is?

In this morning's article, I wrote: "This boy put all kinds of personal information up online, including a photograph, but abducted, he isn't. If he doesn't vanish, then the urban legend of the Headless Rider being a kidnapper will have no legs, in the end."

Just to be clear, confirmed disappeared, he is not.

I will refrain from comments.

In the comment field of the previous article, people who claimed my writing caused his disappearance there were, but true that is not.

If enough time to blame someone you have, then pray for the boy's safety you should do, as an Ikebukuro resident.

Admin: Rira Tailtooth Zaiya

♂♀

A selection of representative twits from the social network Twittia

Man. I wanna sock the admin of IkeNew so bad.

Who puts "Sad News" in an article about a disappearance? Is this a joke to you, Rira?

→There's no use talking to that admin. They make numbers by getting people mad.

→They talk like Yoda in articles about people dying. You think they care?

→And they'll just paste scans of manga right on the top of their articles.

→God, I wish someone would sue IkeNew out of business.

So the Headless Rider got him, right?

→What reason would they have to do that?

→Because he said their favorite food was castella cake bites...?

→ So what? They're yummy.

→ No really, what happens if the Headless Rider is behind these?

→ The IkeNew admin becomes a war criminal for lying that the rider won't hurt anyone.

→ That would mean they were lying when they said it was all lies.

→ Has IkeNew apologized yet?

→ Just don't go there to comment on their blog. It only gives them more hits.

Um, I totally saw the Headless Rider during the daytime today.

→ In Ikebukuro?

→ Talking with Shizuo Heiwajima in West Gate Park.

→ That's definitely her, then.

→ I saw her, too. She was with a girl in middle school or something.

→ Maybe that girl is the next urban legend...

The Dragon Zombie guys are annoying these days, huh?

→ I heard their sickly leader finally got out of the hospital.

→ Sickly?

→ No, he was really weak. But his surgery worked, and now he's better.

→ Horada's back, too.

→ Who's Horada again?

→ Shizuo beat the crap out of Horada a while back.

→ Hey, who's Horada again?

→ Remember that guy who hung off Izumii's ass?

→ Oh, the guy with Higa! Yeah, I remember him!

→Who are you guys? I'll look up your names and whup your asses.

→Who do you think you are? I'm blocking you now.

I've noticed a bunch of cars coming and going from a mansion in the hills near my place.

→You sure they're not coming to see the flowers? It's spring, after all.

→Maybe. Some of them look scary, but others look like students or families.

→Even though school's already in session?

→Huh. That's a good point...

CHAPTER 7

CHAPTER 7 A
The Heir (1)

Yahiro's apartment—night

When Yahiro Mizuchi returned home, the younger brother of his landlord, Saburo Togusa, was working on his van, like always.

"Hey, you're late."

"Sorry about that."

"Don't apologize. I wasn't criticizing. It's not like you have a curfew." Togusa grinned.

Yahiro bowed again. He hesitated briefly, then asked, "Do you know the Headless Rider, Saburo?"

"Huh? Yeah, uh, a bit."

"What's she like?"

"Uh, you mean like her personality...? I mean, I'm not sure she's really a 'person.' But that's not important."

Saburo thought it over for a bit and chose his words very carefully.

"I guess I'd say she's...really nice."

"Nice?"

"Well, the traffic violations notwithstanding—she has no license and drives around without headlights or plates, after all—she's nicer than anyone else. If she saw someone in trouble, she'd help them without a second thought."

He continued waxing the van, clearly enjoying this topic.

"As the guy who has to give other people rides, I thought she was a pain in the ass at first...and I still do sometimes, when she pulls up next to me on the street without warning. But once you understand the reasons why..."

"Reasons?"

"Er...I mean. You know, everyone's got their stuff," Togusa said quickly, trying to move past that. "Anyway, there are lots of folks around here who are scared of the Headless Rider, and she's hurt a couple of thugs, but there are also at least as many folks she's helped out and who feel grateful to her."

"Grateful..."

"You'll understand, if you ever meet her," Saburo said wistfully.

"Oh, I did meet her," Yahiro admitted. "Yesterday."

"You did?!"

"She gave me her e-mail address, too."

"Wow, she's so friendly with you!" Saburo exclaimed, wobbling a little bit. The extra pressure on his wiping hand caused the cloth to squeak. "And what kind of stuff are you getting up to as a high schooler...? Getting beat up by Shizuo Heiwajima, becoming friends with Celty..."

"Oh, so you know Celty's name," Yahiro noted.

"Yeah, I do. I'm sure if you mention Saburo Togusa, she'll remember me." Then he gasped in sudden realization and suggested, "Oh, I know! If you're friends with Celty now, use that to your advantage! She's good friends with Shizuo, so have her patch you guys up."

"She is?"

"Yeah. I mean, if I'm being honest, of all the people I know, she's probably the closest to Shizuo. If you ask her sincerely, I'm sure she'll try to help you out."

"I guess so... I'll ask her about it. Thank you!" Yahiro said, bowing again.

With the wisdom of age and experience, Togusa advised, "Listen, there are lots of weird rumors that get out there on the streets and online. In the end, the only thing you can do is judge what you see with your own eyes. And if you fail, you fail."

"Right."

"The same goes for you, got that? Take good care of your friends.

rumors, but plenty more will look you in the face and judge you based on the real thing."

Yahiro thought that one over for a bit, perhaps because it was hitting home for him. He bowed even deeper.

"...Thank you," he said, a slight smile on his lips. "You must have many wonderful friends, Saburo."

"Ha-ha. Only because I got into too many fights. The truth is, I don't have that many." Saburo smirked, feeling a little embarrassed. He swept his cloth quickly over the van. "Anyway, there are all kinds out there. Like old-fashioned guys who act like the true honorable arbiters of justice or old scalpers who are about as shady as can be... Also..."

His voice trailed away as he saw an anime sticker someone had put on one of the van's rear windows. He envisioned the boy and girl who were certainly the culprits and growled.

"Anyway...take care of your friends. Just be careful about who you pick to be a friend in the first place. Okay?"

♂♀

Yahiro's room

Back in his room, Yahiro lay down on the floor and thought over what Saburo had just told him.

"The only thing you can do is judge what you see with your own eyes."

How did Yahiro appear in the eyes of Himeka, Kuon, and the Headless Rider?

He thought back on older times. Up through middle school, many of the people who attacked him had only heard rumors. After he fought them off, they called him a monster and looked at him with eyes full of fear.

People heard the rumors about him and decided *I'm going to beat him up.* Then, after he beat them, they looked at him in terror. How big was the gap between the rumors and reality for him?

The Headless Rider was much more human than he was led to believe, based on the rumors.

Shizuo Heiwajima was much stronger than he even imagined, and yet he, too, was also much more human than expected.

Shizuo was angry at them because they were insulting the Headless Rider, calling her a kidnapper and making her out to be a freak show. He was angry because his friend was insulted. The reaction was practically noble to Yahiro.

A big part of that was Yahiro's complete lack of friends. His only understanding of friendship came from manga and movies and such.

What would I do? If Kuon or Tatsugami was insulted...would I be as angry as he was? Maybe not, since I've only known them for a few days. But does the length of time really matter? If it does, then maybe I can become friends with them in the days ahead...and even more people than them. Friends as close as Shizuo Heiwajima and Celty the Headless Rider are.

He hadn't actually seen Celty and Shizuo hanging out together, but at this point, Yahiro had no reason to doubt their friendship.

They were two people he'd thought were true monsters—and they *were* monstrous beyond his imagining—but also much more human than he was.

Maybe the rumors were true. But the rumors only told a small part of the story.

"*Lots of weird rumors that get out there on the streets and online,*" he said...

It's true that information can be scary.

Remembering Saburo's advice reminded Yahiro of what happened earlier in the day.

Specifically, what Nozomi Kotonami told him about Kuon.

A few hours earlier—Kuon Kotonami's room

"*Do you know about Izaya Orihara?*"

Nozomi was still talking to them over the phone from her bedroom.

"...No, I'm not familiar," replied Yahiro. He glanced at Himeka, who also shook her head.

"Oh, okay. That makes sense; I'm not surprised you don't know him. Anyway, he's an info broker who's fairly famous around Ikebukuro. He was pretty incredible at it, in fact."

"Uh-huh."

Yahiro was a bit startled by the use of the term *info broker*, but he did feel like the name rang a bell, perhaps.

What is it? I feel like I heard that name recently... Oh.

It was yesterday, when Mr. Ying was talking with the Headless Rider. Someone said it...

But he couldn't be sure if the name he heard was actually Izaya Orihara, so he decided to continue listening and playing the part of the ignorant outsider.

Yahiro and Himeka waited curiously to find out what this info broker had to do with Kuon. The answer stunned them.

"You see, I was a slave of Izaya Orihara."

"Oh...uh...what?" Yahiro gasped. He had initially let the comment pass, until the meaning of the word actually sank in.

"I mean, I can understand now that I was a slave, but at the time, I didn't think it was bad at all. Maybe it was more like I was his true believer."

"True believer...?"

"Me and Kuon grew up without a father and mother. We got abused a lot at the house that took us in. For about half a year, we didn't get any food that wasn't school lunches. Our clothes were used as rags, and then they'd force us to wear them again. And that was the good part. They'd strip us naked together and force us to do things I couldn't repeat here. Not that any of this is especially rare."

"..."

Yahiro was speechless. She was talking about these horrible things as though they were ordinary.

She didn't seem to recognize how much she was freaking him out. Nozomi continued excitedly, *"Anyway, I don't know how he heard about us, but that's when Izaya rescued us."*

"Rescued you?"

"That's right. I was on my way home from school when he called out to me," she said. It sounded like she was about to explain the whole story, but in the very next sentence, she was already at the result. *"Then Izaya*

completely messed up our house. All the people who had tormented us either killed themselves, got arrested, or were abducted and taken somewhere else."

"..."

"We were left behind, and Izaya taught us how to live. Kuon never met him in person, but every single day, I told him how amazing Izaya was. How incredible and wonderful Izaya was. How it was only because of Izaya that we were still alive. That I would do anything for Izaya! That I would happily give my life for Izaya!"

Nozomi was laughing with great elation as she spoke, although neither Yahiro nor Himeka had any idea what was so funny about any of this. They could only stand there and listen.

"Ha-ha-ha-ha! You get it, right? Poor Kuon, he got so jealous of Izaya, even though he never met him. He was so worried about his worthless big sister! You should have seen when I got a boyfriend! He was going on and on about how he was going to kill Izaya."

"A boyfriend...meaning Izaya?"

"No, no! Ah-ha-ha-ha, nooo, I could never be Izaya's girlfriend!" Nozomi denied vehemently. She explained, "You see, there was this street gang called the Yellow Scarves. About four years ago, I talked to some of the senior members of the gang and got to be friends with them. Then we became boyfriend and girlfriend."

But what she said next left both Yahiro and Himeka frowning in consternation.

"Because Izaya told me to."

"...Huh?"

"Saki got to be the girlfriend of the leader of the group, and I got to be the girlfriend of Yatabe, the second-in-command. But actually, he said I could 'do as I liked,' so I went out with the boy for a little while before he dumped me."

"Did you really go out with him, just because this Izaya Orihara person told you to?" Himeka asked.

Nozomi didn't even stop to think. "Yes, I did. I mean, it was only natural. That's how it worked back then."

Back then? Past tense, Yahiro noted.

She laughed again. "After a while, as I did things for Izaya, you can *guess what happened with Kuon, right? I was his only family, and he cared so much for me. He was so sweet. He was like, 'No matter what happens, I'll always protect my sister!'"*

She giggled and cackled, but Yahiro felt like there was just the slightest tremble to her laughter.

"The thing is, I didn't understand."

"Uh…"

"I just didn't understand, you know?" she repeated, her voice sinking deeper.

Yahiro asked, "But…it's different now?"

"…"

Nozomi paused, then gave her answer.

"About a year and a half ago, Izaya vanished."

"He vanished?"

"Yes. He just vanished from Ikebukuro, like a puff of smoke. People said all kinds of things. That Shizuo Heiwajima killed him or that a Russian mercenary stabbed him."

The mention of Shizuo Heiwajima sent a jolt through Yahiro, but he figured that it was just one of many rumors and decided not to interject.

"After that," she continued, *"I just stayed inside all the time. It's funny, but ever since Izaya disappeared, I just don't know what to do. I don't even know how to talk to people anymore. That's why I can only do it over the phone like this."*

It was hard to imagine, based on the gregarious way she was talking now, that she'd been acting the way she was earlier when they were in the same room. But now that he thought back on that, Yahiro felt like he understood her a bit better.

"I feel like I was just in the corner of my room saying, 'Izaya, Izaya, Izaya,'" she murmured uncertainly. Perhaps her memory was hazy. But then she calmed herself a little bit and continued, *"That's when Kuon said, 'I'll be Izaya Orihara.'"*

"Kuon said that…?"

"Yes. He said, 'I'll take Izaya's place and help you learn how to live.'" Nozomi sounded happy but also just a little sad. *"So in the last year and a half, my brother has been trying to turn into Izaya Orihara. No… scratch that. Maybe he's trying to be something even more than Izaya.*

*   *   *

"Whether that's for my sake or his, I don't think either of us knows anymore."

♂♀

Yahiro's room—present moment

He looked up at the ceiling and exhaled.

"The world is full of so many things I don't understand..."

It wasn't even that he was being manipulated by information. It was like he knew barely anything about the world itself.

Yahiro lifted his hand toward the ceiling and made a fist. He stared at it, thinking back on who he'd been until last year.

This is just what the world is like is how he used to think.

He had no hope, no despair. He just lived on inertia.

He felt sick of himself. He was sick of being called a monster regardless of how he struggled against it; he hadn't been able to escape that curse.

But listening to the story of Kuon and his sister today, they seemed to have it far, far worse than he did.

All I did was hurt people, and I blamed it all on others. Was I just sulking? Kuon was hurt over and over and over, and he held it all in and never gave up.

Before, his only mental image of Kuon was of a rather lackadaisical class clown with a bit of a darker secret, but now Yahiro felt actual respect for his classmate.

I'm not saying I think that what he's doing is right...but I'll admit...he is pretty incredible.

He allowed his thoughts to wander as his eyes drifted across the ceiling and around the room, until they landed on the wood-frame radio next to his bed.

Tatsugami seems to have some complicated family circumstances, too. It's possible she's suffered things much worse than my experiences. All I did was get scared of things, while my family was kind and understanding... Maybe I'm just pining for something I don't have.

He started to feel a bit of self-loathing, and stared at one of the newer cuts on his fist.

But even still...

The excitement, the elation he felt while fighting with Shizuo Heiwajima—the feeling that for the first time in his life, the world was fun—still trembled within his fist.

"I'm glad I came to this city," he mumbled out loud, then got to his feet with determination.

With the smartphone he was still learning to use, Yahiro checked the Internet for information. He searched for the disappearances in Ikebukuro, and the first thing that popped up was a news blog called *IkeNew!*

The site that turned the photo of Kuon and Celty into news.

The site run by Kuon's sister.

♂♀

Kuon's room—a few hours earlier

"Well, I managed to get back on my feet. Now I'm running that IkeNew! site I mentioned, along with Kuon. It's managed to bring us an income, enough that we can actually pay rent reliably."

"?"

Yahiro didn't understand the connection between the words *running a site* and *income.*

Despite not being able to see him, Nozomi must have sensed he wouldn't understand, because she began to explain how the site worked.

"So you know how there are banner ads on websites? We get money from the ads."

"Yeah, I guess I do remember a bunch of ads..."

"There are ads that get you paid just from people clicking them and ads that only get you paid when people buy the products there. Also, there are sponsorships and direct partnerships with companies."

"Ohhh."

He'd wondered why there were so many ads on the site, but this cleared it up in quite a neat and tidy answer.

"*Normally, it's just like a little allowance. You'd be lucky to get ten thousand yen in a month. But in my case, the recent average is more like two-point-eight million yen per month.*"

"Million...?!"

"*That's a crazy amount for a site of our size. Especially since it's limited to Ikebukuro news... Oh, and that's the total of all my enterprises. That's not the only website I run.*"

"You...you can make that much money online?!"

"*It varies, see? There are places that make twice as much money as me doing legitimate business, and there are places that act corrupt and get shut down for their trouble. Everything varies,*" Nozomi said.

"What do you mean by corrupt?" Yahiro asked.

Something in her voice got ever so slightly more excited. "*The affiliate blogs can be a real nest of vipers! Lots of them are perfectly legit, but plenty will do anything right up to violating the law. Some blogs even engage in a kind of corporate blackmail.*"

"Corporate blackmail?"

That was another term that didn't seem like it had anything to do with online news.

Nozomi cleared it up for him with an example. "*See, first they'll go after a company and demand, 'Sponsor my blog,' or 'Give me priority on your information.' And once the company refuses, they'll report a bunch of news that makes the company look bad, to put pressure on them, like, 'See, you don't want this to happen, do you?' But they can't just say, 'Give me money or information if you want me to stop,' so they have to be coy about the extortion.*"

"That's horrible."

"*The thing is, it's easy to write malicious articles that don't count as defamation. For example, let's say a magazine puts out a digital version of their product, but the price is more expensive than the print copy. So a website writes an article that says, 'This is messed up! How can the digital version that doesn't require paper cost more?!'*"

"?"

Based on that alone, Yahiro didn't understand why that was malicious; it didn't make sense that a digital magazine would cost more than the same thing printed and sold on physical paper.

Nozomi explained, *"But the digital version was a special edition. It came with all kinds of bonus materials that weren't in the print edition—nearly twice as many pages. So it only made sense that this version would cost a bit more than the other."*

"Oh…"

"Of course, the website knew that when the writer made the article and chose not to explain the context. Even though it was a better deal, they created the impression that the digital version was a rip-off. After the article got passed around, people found out the truth and got angry. They went to the website to write comments saying, 'Don't spread fake news!' but that just drove up the website hits and comments. Those raw numbers make it much easier to attract good sponsors."

Yahiro was shocked. There were people who did that sort of thing?

Nozomi just laughed. *"And if they threaten to sue at any point, you just apologize, say you didn't realize your mistake, and delete the article. You just have to gauge your timing right, because if you screw that up, they might actually take you to court, and then you're screwed."*

"Wow…but you don't do anything like that, do you, Nozomi?"

"Oh, we're way worse than that."

"Worse?!"

Yahiro stared at the phone in disbelief.

"Yes," Nozomi admitted. *"What we do is sell article ideas to other sites, so that they can be the first to report them. But how do you get the news before anyone else?"*

Himeka gasped and said, "You *cause* the news…on your own?"

"Biiingo!"

"That's crazy…," Yahiro breathed. But beyond the sound of Nozomi's excitable voice, he noticed something was wrong.

"…?"

"…"

Is Tatsugami…trembling?

The perpetually calm and composed girl seemed to be rattled by the answer she'd just spoken out loud. It was strange to Yahiro, but Nozomi kept talking.

"Anyway, when I mean news, I don't mean like causing crimes, okay? At least, I think! It'll be, like, mysterious flyers dropped all over

Ikebukuro or a drone that looks like a UFO flying over the city. We go out and take the pictures, then post them on a bunch of random Twittia accounts! The creepier it is, the more viral it goes."

Immediately, Yahiro and Himeka recalled Kuon's photo in the article.

"So that article about Kuon this morning was all a setup," Himeka accused.

"Yep, yep! It sure was!" Nozomi said happily. *"In our case, about 30 percent of our content is stuff we do ourselves. Although the articles about twits of celebrities living in Ikebukuro aren't fake. In any case, you should never take our articles seriously! Most of them are fake or misleading."*

"Why do you write them, then?" Yahiro asked.

He'd scrolled through the articles on the site during lunch period, and lots of the news about Celty was extremely negative. First, they treated her like a certified criminal, then flipped around to the opposite viewpoint just as quickly. It was like the site itself didn't have its own consistent voice.

"Because we don't deal in honest, serious articles. Our style is to use catchy headlines and suspicious stories to manipulate people and companies and society into doing whatever we want!"

"But why would you...?"

"Well, partially it's because that makes the most money, but..." She paused, then brought up that name again. *"If Izaya ran his own site, I'm sure it would be something like this."*

"?"

"I use a name online, Rira Tailtooth Zaiya, right? Well, tail is o in Japanese, and tooth is 'ha.' So if you rearrange all those syllables, you get...I-za-ya O-ri-ha-ra."

"Uh-huh..."

So what?

She claimed that she'd gotten over him, but it was clear that her lingering attachment to Izaya was stronger.

Yahiro tilted his head in confusion once again; it was becoming quite a habit since he came to Ikebukuro. But a few seconds later, he regretted his spotty judgment.

"There are lots of others like me."

"...Lots?"

"Izaya created many other girls in the same position that I was... Plenty of them are out there in despair over his absence. I know at least one who was hospitalized for attempted suicide... But those girls figured it out right away. They found the existence of my site and the anagram puzzle I just explained to you."

"Oh..."

So what? he'd thought earlier. Well, this was the truth. Yahiro felt ashamed of himself.

"See, the moment they figured it out, they felt relieved. 'Oh, good, Izaya isn't gone after all. He's still alive; he's just posting online.' Sometimes that's all it takes for a person to decide to live. We're fascinating that way."

In other words, for the sake of her fellow true believers, Nozomi was playing the role of their religious leader, Izaya Orihara.

Considering the meaning of this, Himeka asked the next obvious question: "But doesn't that mean...you've just been...lying to them all this time? And you'll keep doing it from this point on."

"Hmm... If they want to be lied to, they'll let it keep happening," Nozomi said sadly. *"But if they can accept the fact that I'm not Izaya— if they can accept that Izaya's actually gone—they don't need him anymore, do they? I suppose thinking that way makes me feel a bit less guilty."*

Based on her tone of voice, Yahiro got the impression that she was shrugging her shoulders on the other end of the line.

"Either way, it doesn't change the fact that I'm just a big fat fraud.

"I mean, this site is built on fraudulent stories! If they're fooled, it's their fault!"

♂♀

Yahiro's room—present moment

"Ah!"

Looking back through the archive of *IkeNew!* articles, he found some written about himself.

They made me into an article.

Naturally, it was describing his fight with Shizuo Heiwajima. Apparently, people found him interesting because he could potentially beat Shizuo.

They've got the wrong idea—that's for sure! In the end, I was totally helpless…

There was a video taken of him, too, but the resolution on the camera was low, and he couldn't even recognize his own face in the clip.

But Kuon would know who this "mystery combatant" was, obviously. Did he keep the knowledge a secret from his sister?

No. Nozomi knew about me. Would he really hide things like that from her? Oh, geez. We didn't say a single word about that back at his place…

Yahiro exhaled, feeling conflicted. Should he be grateful they hadn't revealed his name online? He *should* have been furious that they were using him to make money, but that wasn't enough reason for him to blow up at them.

Nobody's going to find out based on this video, at least. And I lost in the end, so I'm sure they'll realize I was just an idiot who overstepped his bounds, and forget about me.

He didn't realize that hitting Shizuo at all made him completely abnormal in the eyes of the locals. So the most he thought about Nozomi's article was that it "seemed really exaggerated."

If anything, he was more worried about Kuon, since that green hair showed up much clearer in the video.

Was he all right? Yahiro recalled what Nozomi said.

"Kuon said he didn't have an exact ID on the culprit, but he knew that if they wanted to make the Headless Rider out to be some vicious kidnapper, they wouldn't let him walk free after that. I just didn't expect he would get abducted hours after I put up the article.

"He'll be fine. He set this up knowing how he'd get out of it…

"If you want to be like Izaya, you have to put your life on the line. That goes for me and Kuon.

"I'm sure you have your own thoughts about this, but if you haven't met Izaya yourself, I'm not interested in any lectures.

"I guess I'm fully aware that I'm a terrible person who could easily get stabbed at any moment."

* * *

There was nothing he could say at the time, but now Yahiro felt a little indignant about it.

Did she care nothing for her own life?

She also said something directly meant for Yahiro.

"You don't need to feel responsible for any of this, Yahiro. He only thinks of you as a pawn meant to be used."

That didn't matter to Yahiro.

"I'm going to find him, and I'm going to give him a piece of my mind."

He chuckled to himself and clenched his fists.

And right on cue, his phone began to ring.

"?"

He picked up the call and heard a familiar voice.

"Hey, it's me. Aoba Kuronuma."

"Oh...how can I help you?" Yahiro replied, remembering that they'd exchanged numbers after school.

"Can you leave the house right now?"

"It's the middle of the night. What happened?" he asked skeptically.

Aoba wasted no time in getting to the point. *"Your friend... Tatsugami? She's been kidnapped."*

"Huh...?"

He felt a horrible shiver run up his spine. Ugly sweat began to seep from his pores.

Before he could reply, to suggest that it had to be a joke, Aoba continued, *"I don't know the culprit, but I know where she was taken."*

"?!"

"So what'll it be? Shall we go and save her?"

CHAPTER 7 B
The Heir (2)

A few dozen minutes earlier—Tokyo

Akane was next to a lonely park not quite in the center of the city, a place that she would normally never visit at night.

Even during the day, she didn't have much of a reason to be here—but for some reason, despite Shiki's very recent abduction, Akane found herself heading down this backstreet.

She was looking around as she went, as though waiting to meet someone.

"This should be the place," she muttered to herself. A van pulled up and stopped nearby. "?"

The next moment, a number of men emerged from the van and casually surrounded her.

"You must be Akane, right?"

"…"

She sensed danger from them and reached for a long, thin bag over her back.

But the men just smiled at her and opened the door on the side of the van.

When Akane saw the person inside the van, her eyes went wide.

And then she *smiled with relief* and started walking toward the van on her own.

"Hey, what the hell do you people think you're doing?!" bellowed a man's loud voice before Akane could say a word.

Everyone turned toward the voice and saw a number of men rushing over.

They were clearly yakuza by the look of them, but Akane was not afraid of them. She recognized them as the men who were always with Shiki.

"…!"

The men who got out of the van panicked and jumped back into their vehicle when they saw the newcomers. One of them reached out for Akane, trying to drag her in with him.

"No!" she shrieked, pulling her hand free as she sensed something dangerous in his expression.

"Ugh…"

They slammed the door of the van shut, and it drove off just as the scary-looking men arrived.

"Get back here!" One of the men tried to jump on top of the vehicle, but he failed to reach the roof and tumbled right onto the pavement. Akane and the newcomers were the only people left on the street.

"Mistress Akane, why are you out here so late…?"

"What about you all? Why are *you* here?"

"Er, w-we just happened to be passing by."

The menacing men sent each other rather obvious glances, prompting each other to play along. They didn't expect that Akane would know Shiki had disappeared.

"More importantly, what was happening with you, miss? You were about to climb right into that fishy van…"

"…I know," she admitted uncomfortably. Then she told them the unvarnished truth.

"I saw someone I know inside that van…"

♂♀

Basement garage of Shinra's apartment

"So is that Shijima guy the culprit? Or was he the first victim? It's one of the two, I bet..."

"Dunno. In either case, now that you're back, I'm sure he's going to do something," Libei said to Celty. Despite the fact that he was rapidly becoming involved in the incident, he was acting like outside help, solving other people's problems.

"If he sees me chatting amicably with you, I suppose I'll be a target next, just like that green-headed boy."

"Hmm? What do you mean?"

"Huh?"

"What?"

Libei realized that they weren't quite having the same conversation. A horrible thought dawned on him.

"Oh, wait...do you not know yet?"

"Know what?"

"That green-headed kid got kidnapped, too."

...

...Huh?!

Time stopped briefly for Celty as she grappled with this unexpected fact.

And then, perfectly on cue, a loud incoming ringtone blasted out of her phone.

"Hello? Is that you, courier? If I have the right number, tap the phone twice," came the voice over the phone.

It's Mr. Akabayashi, she recognized. Another Awakusu-kai lieutenant, like Shiki. Despite her confusion over the news of Kuon, she hurriedly tapped the mic on the phone.

"Well, it's an emergency, which is why I called, rather than writing you a message. You see, Akane was very nearly abducted just a little while ago."

...?!

She had just been talking to Akane during the day. Celty's mind was unraveling even more now.

"I know that you were talking with Akane earlier today. I've had the young guys keeping a constant eye on her, as a matter of fact. I know that you're not responsible, and the guys they saw trying to take her

were unfamiliar. *They didn't look like yakuza, but we don't know any-thing else about them,*" Akabayashi explained to set up the situation. "*Now, at the moment, I've got my friends in Jan-Jaka-Jan trailing them on their motorcycles. So my question is this...*

"*Do you want to clear your name by catching the real culprits yourself?*"

♂♀

Tokyo

"*Mr. Horada, we managed to follow them without being spotted... They went into a mansion in the woods in Hachioji.*"

"Nice! Good job. Keep an eye on them there," Horada said to his henchman over the phone. He was in a very good mood.

"*Okay...but it's looking kind of dicey.*"

"How so?" he asked, frowning.

The younger kid sounded pressed. "*There's a bunch of vans here on this spacious lot...and a good number of people going in and out...*"

"What set are they reppin'? W-wait...it's not the Awakusu-kai, right?" Horada asked, knowing that if it was yakuza, he was with-drawing immediately from this plan.

"*No, it's not them...but it's weird. They're not mobsters. There are, like, normal people coming and going... Plus kids in high school and middle school...*"

"What the hell?"

"*But there are seriously a lot of people... I've seen at least a dozen of them on my own.*"

"Damn, really? If it was only the four or five from that van, we could rustle up the boys and take them... But anyway, give me a map of the area or whatever and e-mail it over," Horada said and ended the call.

Almost immediately, another person was on the line. It was one of his friends from his Blue Squares days. This person was watching the kid named Mizuchi on Horada's orders.

"Yo, how'd it go?"

"Uh, well, we found the Mizuchi kid's house…but it's kind of dicey, man."

"What, you too?! Everyone's telling me it's dicey this, dicey that. What the hell is dicey about it?" he snapped with annoyance.

"His apartment building… It's Togusa's house."

"What?!"

"He was polishing up his van out front, talking with the Mizuchi guy."

Togusa had once been a member of the Blue Squares, but he betrayed Izumii, the leader at the time, and joined that Kadota guy in staging a rebellion.

"Wait a sec, are you tellin' me Kadota's already taken that kid under his wing?!"

"Uh, I have no idea. I said it was Togusa's apartment, right? What if he's just renting a room there?"

"Rrrgh." Horada scowled, as though he'd taken a bite of something bitter.

Shit, what now? he wondered. *It's one thing to make that Mizuchi kid owe us one, but I don't want Kadota involved. How do I make him grateful to me once we know the girl's safe, without getting my hands dirty? For one thing, it's kinda dangerous to try to raid a group when you don't even know who they are…*

He went over all the information he possessed as quickly as he could—and came to one solid conclusion.

That's it. This is what the Blue Squares are for. I'll send them in, and if it turns out to be bad, I can just pretend I didn't know about it. If everything works out, and I get Mizuchi into the Blue Squares, I'm golden. Then I can just go to where they hang out and be like, "Hey, I'm the one who found where they were keeping your girlfriend." That's not a lie, so the current Blue Squares can't complain about that, yeah?

With all these very self-serving thoughts in mind, Horada hit the call button on his phone. *And I just gotta pray that Izumii doesn't show up,* he added, feeling a shiver in his spine.

When the boy answered the phone, he affected a very pleasant tone and said, "Hey! Is that Aoba Kuronuma? It's me, man! You know, me! Your friendly friend Horada! I got a juicy tip here that I figured you kids in my old gang would want to know about!

*   *   *

"There's this big rookie in town—they say he can hold his own against Shizuo Heiwajima. And I want to get him in my debt!"

♂♀

Basement room—Tokyo

It had been over half a day since they were locked in the basement room, but Shiki and Kuon were still calm.

Shiki's subordinate complained every now and then, but a silent glare from his boss immediately restored his fortitude each time.

The two sides did not say much to each other, either to keep their secrets close to their chests or to avoid the guard overhearing what they had to say. So time passed, slowly and silently.

As far as the bathroom was concerned, that was the one time the guard would undo the bonds on their feet, then blindfold them all the way to the bathroom. Once they were inside, the guard would wait on the other side of the door. But as far as their stomachs went, they hadn't been given even a single drop of water to drink.

Based on the bathroom interior and the general sense of the walk to get there, Shiki suspected that they were indeed in some kind of mansion. He attempted conversation a few times, but the guard always said he couldn't talk.

This wasn't the way of his line of work, Shiki decided.

Everything about the way these people were holding them hostage struck him as amateurs trying to fake it with brute force. If they were real amateurs, there was no reason for them to be abducting people, but based on the information he'd gathered, Shiki was close to a conclusion.

He was going to test that hypothesis.

"Hey, kid," he said to Kuon.

"Yes? What is it?" asked the boy politely. His manner had changed once he learned the other man was a yakuza.

But Shiki could see through the false show of respect. He'd made ample use of Izaya Orihara over the years, and everything about the boy, from his attitude to his way of speaking, was extremely similar to the info dealer. Izaya wasn't quite as flippant, but they both shared that sense of sardonic malice lurking beneath the surface, the sheen of smug superiority.

"When you first showed up, you said something about Aya and Ai Tatsugami being here."

"Yes, I did."

"So *which* are they?"

"Which...? What do you mean?" Kuon asked.

But Shiki was in no mood for games. He snapped, "Are they here because they were abducted, like us? Or were they...?"

"If you're far enough along to ask that question, you don't really need me to answer it, do you?" Kuon chuckled awkwardly.

There was some noise outside the door, so Shiki and Kuon paused and glanced toward the entrance. "Oh...do we have a new guest?" Kuon said.

Appearing before them was a teenage girl whose hands and feet were tied up in the same way as theirs. She was also wearing the same uniform as Kuon, making it clear she was a student at Raira Academy.

"Oh? Himeka!" Kuon exclaimed.

"...Kotonami. I'm glad you're all right," said the girl when they took off her blindfold. Her expression was completely flat.

"Look, it's our emotional reunion, so the least you could do is get tears in your eyes and say, 'I'm so glad you're alive!' or something, right?"

"I'm sorry. There's no guarantee we're getting out safely..."

"Well, when you apologize like that, it really starts to sound like we should be worried, so let's not do that, okay?"

"Your sister was worried," Himeka said.

Instantly, the smile vanished from Kuon's face. "...You saw her?"

"The two of us met her," Himeka said, choosing her words carefully to avoid mentioning the name Mizuchi where anyone else could hear.

It wasn't just the kidnappers she was worried about. The man tied up right next to Kuon was clearly not an ordinary civilian, going by the fierce look in his eyes, so she judged that it was safest not to mention any names.

Kuon was silent for a few seconds, then exhaled and shook his head.

"Oh, geez... I can't believe she opened the door for anyone other than the delivery person she knows."

"I'm sorry. Was that invasive?"

"No, it's fine. If she let you in, I have no right to complain about it."

Himeka chose to mention only the result and not the fact that she had pried the lock open. "She said you were abducted with a plan in mind... Do you already know who's responsible?"

"...Wow, how much did she tell you?"

"...She told us about Izaya Orihara."

"..."

Izaya Orihara.

The mention of that name caused Shiki to raise an eyebrow.

But the kids weren't watching him closely enough to observe that reaction.

"...Wow, really? So she told you a lot," Kuon said. He smirked, his eyes cold and dead, and continued, "Then I guess I don't need to keep up the act anymore."

He gazed at her not in his usual lighthearted way but with eyes like a snake watching its prey.

"In fact, I have a question for you, Himeka: *How did you figure out who was responsible?*"

"I always had a bad feeling about it. A sinking sensation that I knew the answer. And to be totally honest, from the point that I learned the Headless Rider was nice... I knew there was no other possibility," she said. She was as blunt as always, but her voice was ever so slightly weaker than usual. "Even still, I wanted to believe. I was ready for this outcome...but a part of me still wishes it were all a mistake."

Of the two grown men who'd been listening to the whole conversation, the bald-headed one shouted, "What the hell are you two talkin' about over there?! Explain it for us, too!"

The other man, who appeared to be his superior, used his trussed-up feet to stomp on him.

"Gwugh!"

"Shut up. You're the only one in the dark."

"Huh? Wh-what do you mean, Mr. Shiki?!" wailed the bald-headed man.

Kuon just smiled at him coldly. "It means the first victims of this incident are *you two*."

"...Huh?"

"Then me, and now this girl is the latest victim."

"What the hell are you talking about?! From what we've learned, at least fifteen people have been abducted!" the bald man shouted.

Shiki replied, "They weren't abducted. We've had the wrong idea about this case from the start."

"What? Wh-what's that supposed to mean, Mr. Shiki?!"

"The people who vanished weren't abducted by the Headless Rider. They just disappeared and lay low to make it look that way."

"...?"

His subordinate looked baffled. Shiki was going to elaborate—but the door opened, cutting him off.

"Well? Have you calmed down a little?"

The woman who appeared in the doorway smiled down at Himeka, who was tied up on the floor.

Himeka answered with absolutely neutral emotion. "I've been calm from the very start. Can *you* say you're actually calm?" Then she paused and enunciated very clearly so everyone else could hear, "Well, *Aya*?"

♂♀

Chuo Expressway

A van drove down the highway toward the Hachioji area.

It did not belong to the kidnappers.

This was one of the Blue Squares' vehicles, owned by an adult member of the group.

Aoba Kuronuma sat in one of the seats, rocking to the vibrations, deep in thought.

I can't believe that Horada guy learned something before I did. Was I overlooking his capability…? He's more talented than I realized.

Aoba didn't realize that Horada had discovered the enemy's base through sheer coincidence and momentum, and it was wreaking havoc on his mental image of the man.

He normally sat in the passenger seat, but today he was in the back seat. He turned to the younger boy sitting next to him and said, "I didn't actually think that you would come along with me, Mizuchi."

"Why not? My classmate was abducted. Of course I want to help."

"…You know, sometimes you're really adrift from the rest of the world. Normally, you'd leave something like this up to the police," Aoba observed. It was a reasonable notion.

Yahiro considered it and answered, "I suppose that's a good point. Why aren't you reporting it to the police?"

"We've all got marks on our records. We don't need to interact with the police any more than absolutely necessary. And I doubt they'd jump into major action based on an anonymous tip." He grimaced. In this case, he was willing to be brutally honest. "We're not running a charity. So if we can find a weakness of this group before it becomes a criminal matter, we can have our way with them. And speaking of which, I find it incredible that you didn't even *think* of the police as an option until I brought it up."

"I've spent so much time being a hassle for the cops, I try not to bother them at all."

"Ah, I see," murmured Aoba. He decided to play one of his cards. "No good memories of the police back in Haburagi Village?"

"…"

Yahiro had no response. He turned slowly to look at Aoba.

For his part, Aoba kept his eyes on the scenery outside the window. "Sorry, I'll admit it: I looked you up. Sounds like you were quite the troublemaker back home. Some of those people still haven't been able to leave the hospital, their legs are broken so badly."

"..."

Aoba was enjoying himself now. He turned to look right at Yahiro. "So why did you come to Ikebukuro? Got tired of the people back home and came to Tokyo for tougher opponents? Like, say, Shizuo Heiwaji..."

His words stopped partway.

Yahiro didn't *do* anything to Aoba. He just met the boy's eyes.

"..."

But that was enough to stop Aoba from speaking.

It felt as though the temperature in the car had dropped several degrees.

Aoba felt as if bottomless darkness had suddenly appeared right before his eyes.

Yahiro Mizuchi's eyes were dark and clouded, completely unlike just moments before.

Instantly, Aoba realized that he was effectively making a tightrope walk between two high-rise buildings. One step out of line and he would be plunging into an unfathomable disaster.

"Kuronuma," Yahiro said without inflection. It sounded like he could very well utter the words "please die" next and try to break Aoba's neck.

But Aoba wasn't so weak-willed that he'd cower in fear in this situation.

"What is it?" He smiled.

"The guy whose arms and legs I broke...hit me with a *dump truck*."

"..."

"He was driving it without a license. After hitting me, a bunch of them came attacking me with pickaxes... So even after everything I did to him, I got off on justified self-defense," Yahiro said, as flat and plain as though he were reading it out of a journal.

Aoba doubted that self-defense was really a valid defense in this case, but he wisely chose not to say anything. That was a distinction that did not matter in the scope of what Yahiro was talking about.

"Today, they try to kill me with a dump truck. What if they drive it into my house next time? What if my family dies? I couldn't help but be terrified."

"…And then?"

"And then I thought, *The answer is to make sure he can never drive a truck again*," Yahiro stated.

Aoba felt a shiver tickle his spine. Not a chill of fear but more of a trickle of delight at the sheer alienness of the person he was sitting with.

Uh-huh. So this is Yahiro Mizuchi.

…Fascinating.

"So were you assuming that I was fighting just to waste time and keep from being bored…?" the boy asked, looking conflicted. Aoba said nothing, so he went on, "I've never engaged in a single fight just for f…"

But he didn't complete the word *fun*. He'd just had a flashback to his fight with Shizuo Heiwajima and the sensation when Shizuo's fist hurtled toward his face.

It was a tremendous punch, sheer trauma incarnate.

But even then, there was something different about that fight. He could say that for certain.

If asked why, Yahiro would find it difficult to put the reason into words at that moment. He was rattled at the time, too, and he could sense it was an opportunity for him to finally break out of being treated like a monster and turn into something else instead.

But Yahiro knew that his opportunity was shadowed by dark storm clouds.

Oh…I get it. It's going to end up in a shambles, isn't it?

In the last few days, he'd come to understand that Aoba Kuronuma was not actually the pleasant, polite person he appeared to be. But he hadn't imagined that Aoba would look into his past and try to drag it here, into Yahiro's life in Ikebukuro.

Even here, I can't escape it.

But it was only natural that this would happen. He was able to look up the Headless Rider and Shizuo Heiwajima from home. Of course, people in Tokyo could look up his past, too. It was just evidence of the enormity of what he'd done in his hometown.

Yahiro felt shame envelop him and closed his eyes.

"…I'm sorry. I got a little emotional."

Then he looked away from Aoba and out the window. The orange lights over the highway illuminated the plaintive look on his face.

What am I going there to do? To save Tatsugami? Do I even have the right? How does a monster like me save other people…?

Thoughts and memories of the past shot through his head.

So many different people and the looks in their eyes. Watching him. Always.

He wanted to turn away from all of it, unable to bear their gazes.

I can't. I have to get past this, or I'll never change. I just need a chance, the right opportunity to be different. Something that provides a path that I can take the first step down—whether forward or backward.

He clenched his fists and prayed. Not to any god or devil in particular—he just prayed.

And then…

A shadow.

A sudden and unprompted anomaly shut down Yahiro's train of thought.

…?!

Despite the presence of the orange highway lights and the headlights from the cars behind it, an object of pure darkness passed right before Yahiro's eyes—to the side of the Blue Squares' van.

"The Headless Rider…?"

"Hey, Aoba! What's going on? Did you contact the Headless Rider, too?!" yelped the driver.

"No," Aoba replied, "I was going to, once we had confirmation…but I didn't do anything yet."

"I've seen that bike, leading the way in front! That's someone from Jan-Jaka-Jan!"

"Uh-huh. So has the Awakusu-kai figured something out?" Aoba muttered, with no small frustration. But then he noticed something. "Hmm…?"

A number of bikers dressed in white riding suits were following Celty from a short distance behind.

"Are those guys…Dragon Zombies?!"

It was a very strange formation cruising down the expressway, black followed by a flock of white.

Aoba realized that they, too, were part of that mysterious flow and felt glee pulling up the corners of his mouth.

"This is gonna be rowdier than I imagined.

"In a sense, we're lucky we didn't show up late to the festival."

♂♀

Himeka Tatsugami didn't think of herself as misfortunate.

Neither had she ever felt that she was fortunate.
So was her life one of happiness or misery?
She had no answer to that.

She was a strong person—not in terms of physical strength or in great intelligence. Her mental fortitude, though, had been squarely ahead of the pack all throughout her life.

Even at a young age, she never cried or wailed at the haunted house attractions, and she never screamed on a roller coaster.

If asked for her opinion, she would say it was "really scary," but when it came in such a neutral tone, few people ever believed her.

For as long as she could remember, she had simply accepted the reality around her on a continual basis.

She accepted her father screaming at her mother, his face red and terrifying. She accepted that he punched strangers.

She accepted the warmth of his palm when he rubbed her head with a smile, a completely different person.

She accepted the knowledge that he was a criminal when her little sister was born.

She accepted that her father ran a lending business that charged illegal interest rates. In other words, that he was a loan shark who ruined the lives of others.

She accepted that when she was still in elementary school, her big sister told the police about what his company did, hoping they would arrest him.

She accepted that she was hazed by her classmates because of her father's arrest.

She accepted that she brushed off all the nasty pranks and rose above them, giving her one of the strongest positions in the class.

She accepted that the kids who had bullied her were now sucking up to her, trying to win her favor.

She accepted that after her father was gone, her mother slowly fell apart.

Despite the fear he instilled with all of his screaming, did her mother really love him? Or did she simply confuse fear-based loyalty with love?

Himeka couldn't understand it, and it was something between the two of them, not her, so she never felt the need to ask about it.

In either case, to fill the sense of loss she felt, Himeka's mother created her ideal world within her own shadow and spent her time speaking to the darkness in the wall.

Within that fictional reality, her mother apparently suffered not just her father's yelling but also his violence. Whenever she called out Himeka's or her sisters' names, she would mutter, *"Don't leave me here. Don't leave me alone with him."*

Why, in her imaginary world, did she imagine even worse treatment than she suffered in reality? Was *that* her ideal existence? Himeka didn't understand it—but even then, she accepted her mother and cared for her the way anyone would love their mother.

And by that token, though Himeka understood and identified her father as absolute scum, she loved him the way anyone would love their father, too. She hoped he would reform his ways in prison and emerge a changed man, and she wanted to do her part to support his return to society.

Where Himeka miscalculated was that she failed to realize just how strong she was.

Because of that, she assumed her sisters faced all these things and accepted them in the same way that she did.

All until the moment she heard her older sister curse the world itself.

Around the time Himeka started middle school, one of her father's former clients stabbed her sister, who was in college.

When the police questioned him, he lamented that people suspected him of leaking the information to the police, and no other loan sharks would loan him money anymore.

The man was the owner of a small workshop and had run out of goodwill with the banks and turned to black market money in an emergency. But the rumors about him led to the bankruptcy of his workshop and his own ruin. In his fury, he turned to violence.

Aya and the workshop owner knew each other, and it was true that she had turned over the records of his dealings to the police. Naturally, she couldn't have known that it would lead to something like this.

What Himeka didn't know until later was that there were plenty of people who knew loan sharks charged illegal rates but made use of their services anyway.

But by the same token, she did not think of loan sharks as a necessary evil.

Their father pursued only his own enrichment—it was true—and that might have helped this workshop owner, but it also meant that many more people did not recover from his loan schemes and fell into ruin.

Therefore, Himeka didn't think her sister was wrong to do it, and if the workshop owner was going to blame anyone, he should blame the stingy banks or the bad economy, not Aya.

So Himeka was terribly disturbed by her sister's stabbing, but she used sheer willpower to overcome the shock and helped take care of things to support her sister.

"Why did this happen to me? I did the right thing. Didn't I, Himeka?"

She did. *She did the right thing*, Himeka thought.

So Himeka said just that. *"You did the right thing, but the right thing isn't always rewarded. Maybe that's just how the world works.*

"I won't state for certain that there are no gods or higher powers out there. Maybe they do exist, but they certainly don't reward people immediately for doing the right thing. So stick with us, and we'll keep going together."

That was what she said, honestly and openly, but her sister's response was different.

*   *   *

"...I can't believe you can be so cruel. Do you know what Mom said when she talked to the wall like that? She said, '...Don't turn your father in to the police. We're a family.'

"Is that the right thing to her? Is it the right thing for her to say that to me?

"I hate it. I can't think the way you do. I can't look at the world with cold, enlightened eyes like yours and just give up on everything."

Her sister's words dug deep into Himeka's heart.

It wasn't that those words were truthful.

Himeka never thought of herself as having a cold attitude, and she specifically didn't want to give up on everything because of all the pain she was in.

So it was unbearably sad to her that her sister viewed her as the inverse of what she was.

But because Himeka was sturdy by nature, she withstood that sadness. She didn't break down and cry or rage with indignance. She just continued to help her injured sister get by.

To others, however—even her own mother and sisters—that toughness just appeared freakish.

She has no emotions, people often thought mistakenly.

She had a mental sensitivity just as rich as anyone else's and the full range of human emotions.

When she enjoyed something, she smiled—just like anyone else.

But for her, there was much more time spent withstanding sorrow and pain than feeling delight.

Because of that, she was rarely moved by anything, and she could easily contain the most blistering anger and hold back tears of sadness.

The lack of outward emotion was not at all a sign of flimsy humanity. Himeka Tatsugami's problem existed before any of that.

For better or worse, she was simply too strong at withstanding any kinds of emotional swings.

And that strength caused an unintended drift. She fell out of touch with the sisters she cared about more than herself.

Her little sister Ai, too, was not strong enough to withstand the cascading effects of such a cold reality: the troubles stemming from her father's arrest, the unfairness of her sister's stabbing for doing the right thing, her mother's mental collapse.

Her big sister recovered and left the hospital, but the time she spent there left her falling behind in setting up a job after school, another reminder of the cruel nature of reality.

One day, she was watching TV and muttered, "Headless…Rider…"

Nobody who'd lived in Ikebukuro for years would hear that name and not know what it meant.

Himeka was startled the first time she saw the silent motorcycle, but her initial impression was simply that it was a strange, berserk rider on a strange, berserk motorcycle.

She wasn't the only one who felt that way. Many Ikebukuro residents thought of it as nothing special at the time.

Until one day, when things changed permanently.

The mysterious, unexplained Headless Rider appeared on the TV cameras. It did things that were physically impossible, fashioning a gigantic scythe of shadow from its body and racing straight up the side of a building. It seemed to be trying to impress its existence upon the rest of the world.

Himeka thought it was incredible but couldn't eliminate the possibility that it was just special effects—until the Headless Rider began to use those supernatural powers all the time, during the day, in the presence of crowds.

It was as though the city itself had accepted the rider's existence.

Her older sister would have witnessed that, too. She began to study the Headless Rider with a fervor akin to ghostly possession. She would talk at length about how fantastical, how far outside the bounds of reality it was.

That was when Himeka realized something: This had become something of a religious fervor to Aya.

Aya believed the rider was something that could puncture a hole in the unbreakable, irrational hull of society—something even more irrational from another world entirely.

Maybe it really was a ghost. Or maybe it was some kind of angel or devil.

Once the truth about it was proved, the very model of the world would change.

You wouldn't know if the second hand on a clock was ticking into the future or the past.

Would it be explained with science or worshipped as a holy mystery? In either case, the world would change.

It would take them away from this irrational, unfair world.

That was what Aya believed, whether she had any evidence for it or not.

Even though, whether the Headless Rider was really something beyond the bounds of the world or not, it had not come to *save* anyone.

For one thing, the Headless Rider had apparently been in Ikebukuro for over twenty years. If it was meant to save someone, why didn't it save Aya when the workshop owner stabbed her?

To Himeka, the Headless Rider remained nothing but a stranger with a strange power.

But she wasn't going to expend any energy arguing that point. If the Headless Rider was something that gave her sister the will to go on, then its existence alone was, in fact, serving to save her life.

And she held onto those beliefs—until the Headless Rider disappeared from Ikebukuro.

At first, it was just a rumor, but as the days passed without any sign of the Headless Rider, her sister became more and more desperate.

Himeka even saw her muttering at the wall alone, just like their mother did so often.

"The Headless Rider's going to take us somewhere else. The Headless Rider's going to free us from this world."

And in addition to Aya, Ai was also infected with this devotion. The two of them would even go out to wander the streets in search of the rider.

The Headless Rider brought her sisters hope, then vanished without providing anything else. Himeka knew it was just an emotional response and wasn't fair, but she was decidedly dispassionate on the topic of the rider.

At times, she even entertained the thought that the Headless Rider was an actual demon, bringing people false hope in order to lure them into total despair.

When she realized the kind of conclusions she was making about someone she'd never met in person, Himeka felt disgusted with herself. She was no better than the man who stabbed her sister, and perhaps even worse.

Maybe *she* was the one who was being unfair to the rider. While she didn't let it show on her face, that miserable feeling continued to accumulate within Himeka.

But one day, her big sister's mood was suddenly improved. And after that, her little sister started acting strangely.

Around this time, her big sister often asked, *"Maybe you're right, Himeka, and there are no gods or higher powers in the world. So if there's no god, why don't we make one?"*

Himeka didn't give her a firm answer—she didn't know what Aya meant—but her sister continued absently, *"You don't have to try anymore, Himeka. One day, you'll understand."*

When Ikebukuro lost its famous urban legend, it was Aya who longed for the Headless Rider's return more than anyone else.

Aya vanished a month later—right alongside her younger sister, who was just as fervent about searching for the rider.

Normally, you wouldn't expect someone to be able to keep a rational mind, losing two sisters at the same time. But Himeka had the strength to recover right away, giving her the mental sharpness to come up with a hypothesis.

Was my older sister really kidnapped?

When she saw the unfinished memo the magazine office found left behind, Himeka felt something was off. Her sister had worshipped the Headless Rider, but this was too clipped and emotionless for her. And the information about the rider itself was noticeably *less* than what she talked about at home.

Could it be...?

She had a bad feeling. A possibility had occurred to her.

But she wanted to rule it out.

Regardless of the situation, she wouldn't do something *that* ridiculous.

Himeka loved both of her sisters. If it came to the Headless Rider versus her own family, Himeka decided she would trust her sisters.

And now to the present...

The reunion with her older sister was nearly the worst possible scenario.

If seeing her as a dead body or maimed for life was the actual worst case, then this was the next worst thing.

Here in the basement of this mansion a fair distance away from Ikebukuro, Himeka learned the awful truth: Her sister was not a victim but a perpetrator.

"Hello again, Himeka. How many days has it been?" said her sister, looking down at Himeka on the floor with an empty smile on her face.

Himeka just coldly stared back at her. "We were together in the van ride over here. I just couldn't see you, because I was thrown around on the floor in the back."

"Oh, is that right? Ah…yes, perhaps," said Himeka's sister, Aya Tatsugami, with a gentle smile that did not break. "But regardless, I'm glad you made it here safely. Don't worry—everyone here is very nice."

"…What are you talking about?"

"The Great Celty, the Headless Rider, has returned. It's all okay now."

"Um, Aya?"

Himeka could sense something was wrong. Their conversation wasn't adding up.

"We're going to bear witness to a new age. And you get to be one of those witnesses."

"What are you talking about…? Is Mom all right?"

"Mom? Oh yes, she was talking with the wall in the bathroom. She's fine—she belongs to Dad. Neither you nor Ai needs to suffer for Dad or Mom anymore. This is all thanks to the Great Celty. I'm sure Dad died in some prison somewhere. The Great Celty will rescue Mom at some point. Yes, it's all okay. Everything will go well, and it will all be okay…"

"Stop it… You're just using the Headless Rider as a means of escape. You're only bothering that poor woman," Himeka accused.

Aya's neck nearly twisted itself off as she turned to look at her sister. "Poor woman? You call the Great Celty a *poor woman?*" Her face was still smiling, but there was a boundless chill emanating from it.

"…Yes."

"What would you know about her?"

"Plenty. It's what she said to me," Himeka replied.

The smile vanished from Aya's face.

"…What? What do you mean?"

"Well…," Himeka murmured.

Kuon picked up the slack. "Himeka met Celty with me."

It was a direct challenge.

All time within the room stopped still.

The men standing around Aya were rendered mute by her heavy silence.

"…Why?" she said at last, her voice faint. "Why? Why you?"

"Aya…"

"It makes no sense. This world makes no sense. I have to escape… I have to hurry into the black smoke…," she muttered to herself.

"Stop this, Aya!" Himeka shouted. "I'm certain you didn't start all this! Who dragged you into it at the beginning?!"

"Dragged me…? You're wrong, Himeka. We dredged it up out of that filthy swamp-like place… If you don't believe me, look at what a good mood I'm in. See? You understand, don't you?"

"What…? No, I don't…"

They weren't having a real conversation. Himeka had no idea how to proceed.

Behind her, Shiki said softly, "I don't think you can convince her of anything right now, young lady."

"Huh…?"

"Uh…you might want to steel yourself for this one. I think your sister's on *some kind of drugs*."

"…!"

The steel mask of Himeka's face actually went slightly pale.

"Her eyes, her expression… I've seen this before," he said. "Everyone who tries out the street drug Heaven's Slave ends up like her. They have that withdrawal reaction as soon as anything unpleasant happens to them. They're surrounded by bliss, so they can only see and hear things that are convenient for their mental state."

If Aya felt upset about anything, it was learning that Himeka had come into contact with Celty first, she realized at once. And it was clear that her sister wasn't right.

"Oh no…"

"But it's still early. If you can stop her, she'll recover."

Based on that, Kuon decided to speak up for Himeka while she was still too shocked to react. "Um, hey, are you her sister? Does that mean Ai is all right, too?"

The mention of their sister's name caused Aya to pause briefly. "Ai? Ai…oh! Yes, that's right. Don't worry. I'm sure Ai's doing what she needs to do. She's going to bring that schoolmate of hers who was talking with the Great Celty and Shizuo Heiwajima."

Shiki and his subordinate twitched at that.

"If you'll pardon my question," he asked, "do you know what the name of that schoolmate is?"

"Oh? Who are you? Well, anyway…I think…yes, she said it was Akane."

"…"

"B-Boss!" exclaimed the panicked driver.

Shiki scowled bitterly but composed himself again and calmly asked, "Why is she going after that girl?"

This time, perhaps because it was something "convenient to her mental state," Aya gave a proper answer.

"Shizuo Heiwajima's beyond the bounds of human existence, so he has the right to talk to her. But no normal girl can possibly be allowed to consort casually with our hallowed deity," she said, grinning. Then she kicked Kuon in the head.

"*Gah…!*"

"Stop it, Aya!"

"It's all right, Himeka. I'm not going to kill him. I just want him to regret his mistake…and then have him disappear," Aya said forebodingly. But Himeka didn't give up.

"And then…you're going to make sure that gets blamed on Celty, too, like all the others?!"

Aya craned her neck, mystified by Himeka's statement.

"What do you mean? The Great Celty will make *everyone* disappear. We understand the will of the Great Celty. And our will is the Great Celty's will."

"…"

"After the Headless Rider vanished from Ikebukuro, we protected her legend. It's only a series of disappearances now, but soon everyone will start spreading rumors. Rumors that the people taken away by the Headless Rider are passing through shadow into a world without pain."

She was making absolutely no sense and wasn't hearing them. And the look on her face said she wasn't blathering on to disregard their questions, but that she really believed she was speaking the truth.

The sharp, intelligent writer's side of her was completely gone. The Aya here was unrecognizable to Himeka—she was nothing but a cultist drowning in blind faith.

Himeka looked away slightly but accepted this horrible reality at face value.

She's wrong. But I'm not going to just run away from her or Ai. I'll never run away from reality...or from the Headless Rider, she swore.

"Aya, I'm begging you," she said. "You need to actually meet the Headless Rider and have a conversation with her. I'm sure you'll understand after that."

"I'm fine, Himeka. We're already so, so happy right now. When you create and spread an urban legend, you fall under this illusion that you're part of that very legend—according to what a senior writer told me. And it's true. It's *not* an illusion. I'm already a part of the Headless Rider," Aya reveled, joyful madness in her eyes.

Himeka stared at her, accepting the sight. But before she could say her next words, the door to the room opened, and a man entered to whisper something into Aya's ear.

"...She did?" Aya murmured and hurried for the door. "I'm sorry, Himeka. Apparently, Ai failed to kidnap that Akane girl."

"Huh?"

Himeka's eyes were big and round. Behind her, Shiki exhaled with relief.

"But don't worry. I'll make sure to succeed this time."

"Wait, Aya..."

But Aya slammed the door shut, leaving only the one guard behind.

As though she were running away from the reality Himeka was speaking of.

♂♀

Hachioji

"*...I didn't expect I'd be meeting you like this.*"

After she received the message from Yahiro Mizuchi, Celty headed a short distance away from where the Awakusu-kai figures were gathering to meet up with the boy.

"I'm sorry. All this took me off guard, too."

"So why here?"

"The truth is…"

Once Yahiro had explained the situation, Celty's shoulders slumped.

"Aoba Kuronuma—where did he get that information?" she asked, but she knew that the boy had an information network comparable to Izaya's. Perhaps he'd tapped the Awakusu-kai somehow. She decided it was best not to think too hard about it.

"Anyway," she continued, *"what are you planning to do? Are you going to raid the kidnappers with Aoba and his friends?"*

"Two of my friends are being held hostage. I can't just leave them there."

"Well, given my position, I can't just tell you to let the police handle it…but there's no need for you to expose yourself to danger, too."

"It might not be necessary, but I still feel like I *need* to be here. Let me help," Yahiro said. He knew that he wasn't being fair or rational, but he couldn't back down now. "If I stop here, this opportunity I've started to grasp is going to slip away from me…"

"Opportunity?" Celty asked.

Yahiro panicked and shook his head. "A-anyway, I know I'm not necessarily being rational. But…if Kuon and Tatsugami were kidnapped, I might be their next target. I think I could serve as good bait."

"Well, I'll admit that I didn't think Himeka would get abducted, too…"

If Yahiro were just an ordinary teen, she would easily override him because of the danger, but Celty was aware by now that Yahiro was anything but ordinary.

He was like a milder version of Shizuo Heiwajima. She might not need to stop him from getting into a fight, but the problem was they didn't know who the other side was. It could turn out to be the kind of people who came out guns blazing when the action started.

On top of the hot-blooded members of the Awakusu-kai, you've also got Dragon Zombie in the mix…

And then add the Blue Squares, for good measure. Dragon Zombie and the Blue Squares were not on good terms at all. And between true rivals like Dragon Zombie and Jan-Jaka-Jan, one wrong move could send the relationship spiraling into a turf war.

And these are the people who attempted to kidnap Akane, the grand-daughter of the head of the Awakusu-kai. They aren't going to show mercy. They could very well have guns on them right now, Celty thought, focusing on the negative possibilities. She shook her helmet to clear her mind.

"*What's your goal here?*" she asked Yahiro.

"Huh?"

"*There was a boy who came to Ikebukuro in search of the abnormal. When he made his way to the underside of society, I didn't stop him. At this point, I don't know if that was a good idea or a bad one. In the end, he got badly hurt and withdrew from this side of things. If you have a real purpose in mind and you get hurt, that's on you. But I wouldn't recommend getting involved with this if you're just being swayed by a momentary emotional swing.*"

She was reminiscing on some rather vivid memories from the recent past that could have relevance with the boy she now faced.

"*Tell me,*" she continued. "*Did you come to this city with a certain determination in mind, a goal you wanted to achieve?*"

Yahiro was silent for a while. Then he looked right back at her and said, "Celty."

"*What is it?*"

"...I'm going to say something extremely rude. Something I deserve to be punched for saying."

"*Um, I'm not going to punch you for asking a question...,*" she typed, tilting her helmet in bewilderment.

Yahiro took a deep breath and steeled his courage for the confession he was going to make.

About why he had come to this place.

About what people called him back home.

"How does it feel...to have everyone call you a monster?"

♂♀

Mansion basement

"Oh no, what should I do? I have to do something, or that poor Akane girl will..."

Himeka was crestfallen by the fact that she wasn't able to talk sense into her sister, but true to form, she muffled that sadness and focused on practical matters.

Behind her, Shiki said, "Your sister and her friends aren't going to get a second chance."

"?"

Kuon sensed her confusion and answered in Shiki's stead. "Most likely, the Akane she mentioned is Akane Awakusu. She's the granddaughter of the boss of the Awakusu-kai."

"...You know a lot, kid," Shiki muttered.

"I go to the same dojo as her."

"...Oh, so you're with Rakuei Gym," he said, the pieces clicking into place.

Kuon nodded and lowered his voice so the guard couldn't overhear. "Meaning...the people here at this mansion have made mortal enemies of the Awakusu-kai."

Shiki picked up from there. "Mistress Akane's had someone keeping an eye on her. So you can assume that whoever attempted to kidnap her is being trailed at the moment."

"Uh, meaning..."

"There are several Awakusu men on their way here right now, young lady."

"..."

Himeka looked conflicted about this. Her relief at the prospect of rescue was being outweighed by concern that her sister was making enemies of the yakuza.

"Hey, what are you whispering about over there?" asked the guard suspiciously, noticing that they'd been muttering under their breath to one another.

"Oh, I'm sorry about that," said Shiki. "We were worried that the floor was going to be stained with blood."

"Blood?" the man repeated, coming closer.

He really was an amateur. He walked right in between the four of them to examine it, without a care in the world.

That was when the base of Shiki's palm smashed the bridge of his nose.

"*Brguh...*"

Blood spurted from his nostrils as his head shot backward.

At some point, Shiki had worked his limbs free of their binding. He leaped to his feet and grabbed the man's right wrist and head, lifting firmly.

"And now..."

"Aieee!"

He had the man's wrist pinned behind his back and yanked hard on his hair. Then, manipulating the man's center of gravity, Shiki smashed his face against the corner of the shelf.

"...!"

The man exhaled in a silent scream. Shiki grappled with him again, this time slamming his face directly against the ground. There was an ugly *crunch*, telling the others that the man's nose was thoroughly broken. The unconscious man's face bled profusely onto the floor.

"See? Now it's stained, isn't it?" Shiki commented.

Kuon's mouth fell open with shock. "When did you get loose...? Huh...?"

"I could have worked my way free at any time, but I decided to stay put until I knew who they were. We make a living tying people up. You think I can't see through amateur work...?"

"Um, excuse me...," interrupted Shiki's bald subordinate, while his boss felt around for his victim's smartphone. "Mr. Shiki...? I couldn't get loose. Could you help me...?"

♂♀

Outside the mansion

"*I see. And that's why you were looking for me and Shizuo...,*" Celty typed, showing Yahiro the words on her screen. "*Do you think Shizuo is a monster?*"

"...In terms of strength."

"*And outside of strength?*"

"...He was nice."

Inside her mind, Celty whistled. There were very few people she'd ever met who could take punches from Shizuo and immediately say he was "nice" when asked.

"He was angry on behalf of you and his brother. The way he was angry for his friends, rather than himself, just seemed incredible to me."

"*That's true.*"

Although he's also getting mad because of himself all the time, too, she thought, but it wasn't worth derailing the conversation, so she let him continue.

"He's been called a monster by so many more people than I have, but he lives such an honest, straightforward life… It made me wonder what I should do to be more like him…"

Straight…forward…?

All she could think of were the street signs and postboxes that Shizuo had destroyed. It seemed like the boy was overestimating Shizuo's nature, but again she didn't contradict him. She was a serial traffic violator, so she had no room to talk.

"It made me think, maybe I'm not actually alone, after all… That if I came to Ikebukuro, I could talk with other people who've been called monsters and find an actual reason for me to live… I'm sorry—I know it's presumptuous."

"*No, you don't need to apologize. It's true that people see me as a monster, after all,*" she said and then took her helmet right off her shoulders.

"!"

The only thing underneath it was the cross section of a neck, from which that black shadow exuded.

Yahiro was alarmed at the suddenness of it all, but once he got his breathing under control, he said, "You really…aren't human."

"*You're not frightened.*"

"No, my knees are knocking," he admitted, swallowing hard. He clenched his fists and opened his mouth to exhale. What really frightened him was not Celty's headless appearance—it was the fear he felt when being faced with his own insignificance in the presence of the real thing.

"I suppose it must really annoy you to be lumped in with posers like me, who only get called monsters because of the things we do."

"*Why not be one?*"

She thrust the smartphone under his chin as he tried to bow in apology, forcing him to stop.

"…Huh?"

"If you don't want to be a poser, you should try just being a monster."

That was a suggestion that the Celty of just a few years ago would never have made.

"Don't be afraid of becoming a monster."

There was a time in Celty's life when she was much more fixated on the thought that she wasn't human. She created a rift between herself and all humanity.

"Even if you wound up with a headless body like mine...you're still you."

That rift hadn't vanished because she decided to be human. It was because she'd been blessed with a very fortunate encounter.

"The world is so much bigger than you think. Believe in your life... Well, I probably shouldn't say that—it's too grandiose. But whether you turn into a monster or not, somewhere out there are people who will believe in you and people who will love you."

She was thinking of the face of the man who gave her his purest affection—love for a monster. It was the face of the man she gave her purest love to in return.

"People...who will believe in me?"

"As long as you don't stop believing in that person you'll meet some-day, you're a human being, you're a monster...

"And you're always Yahiro Mizuchi."

"Ah..."

For just an instant, Yahiro thought he saw the headless woman smile.

Just that little illusion was enough.

The Headless Rider's smile was the best possible opportunity for him to move forward than he could possibly have hoped for.

Mansion basement

Shiki untied his bald subordinate and ordered him to free Kuon and Himeka, after which Shiki turned on the unconscious guard's smartphone and used the maps application to check their present location. Using that address, he did an online search to identify the real estate listing of the building they were in.

"What a convenient age we live in," he muttered, looking at a title that said *Mansion, Owner: Shijima Realty*.

Apparently, all the properties in this area were owned and sold by the Shijima Group. He remembered that name.

I see now. So that's why I got captured. Shijima was the only one dealing Heaven's Slave…so when I was investigating the Headless Rider's case, they caught sight of me and figured it was two birds with one stone.

By abducting a mobster like Shiki, Shijima could make the public think the Headless Rider was finally going after the Awakusu-kai, and he could also get revenge against the man who crushed his drug-dealing operation.

But why now? Using the Headless Rider's worshippers as a front to bring back his old operation…? Is he really stupid enough to try that with a group of amateurs?

If it was really Shijima doing all this, he should probably have come to finish off Shiki himself by now.

The questions kept flowing through Shiki's mind, but he decided he didn't have enough information on hand to reach a conclusion. He shifted his thoughts to the near future instead.

First of all, he'd use the smartphone to contact his direct superior in the gang, Mikiya Awakusu. Shiki had the numbers of all the central officers memorized just for situations like this, so he dialed the number directly and placed the call.

"…*Who is this?*" Mikiya said upon answering, suspicious of the unfamiliar number.

"I'm sorry, Mikiya. It's me."

"*Shiki?! Where are you now?!*"

"In Hachioji. I've slipped in among the kidnappers. Is the mistress safe?"

"*I just got word that she'd nearly been taken. Your men chased them off. I'm grateful.*"

It was a very brief thanks, but Shiki didn't mind. He explained his situation to Mikiya but did not mention Aya or her sister, out of respect for Himeka, who was nearby.

"A couple of them are junkies, but I'd bet Shijima is the one behind this operation. Right now I mean to find out if there's someone else manipulating him even further in the shadows."

"Akabayashi's pet bikers and the youngbloods under Aozaki's wing are heading there now. Be careful you don't get caught in the cross fire," Mikiya warned.

Shiki's brow furrowed. "Aozaki's not giving them weapons, is he?"

Aozaki's faction was the most aggressive in the Awakusu-kai. They were all short-tempered and itching to fight, including Aozaki himself. If they started shooting civilians—even junkie civilians—it could spell the end of the Awakusu-kai itself.

"We just have to trust he'll be rational about it. If I could, I'd raid that place myself right now."

"I'll do my best not to make things worse," Shiki promised. After a few more traded comments, he ended the call and turned back to Kuon and Himeka. "We're going to head outside now. I think you're better off not leaving this room right now."

"No…I'm going. I'm worried about my sister," said Himeka, crisp and firm. She was not intimidated by the knowledge of Shiki's occupation.

Shiki was impressed, but he had no reason to escort an amateur around. He was starting to worry that he shouldn't have untied them so quickly, when he heard footsteps descending the stairs to the door.

He glanced toward his associate, who nodded and snuck over to the door.

As soon as it opened, the bald man leaped onto the person who walked through—and got knocked clean out, his eyes rolling back into his head.

"!"

Shiki held his breath at the sight of that vivid blow, fierce and accurate to the temple. But before he could worry about the potential danger, he noticed the figure behind the first person through the door.

Aside from the helmet, it appeared to be made entirely out of shadow.

"Tatsugami! Kuon! You're all right!"

As soon as they recognized that it was Yahiro rushing toward them, Himeka's and Kuon's eyes went wide.

"Mizuchi?!"

"Yahiro?! And…Celty?!"

Yahiro was relieved that his two friends didn't seem to be hurt—but no sooner had he felt that relief than the sight of the man standing near them sent a shiver down his spine.

Years of experience and innate instinct were telling him the same thing.

That the man standing there was extremely dangerous—in a different way than Shizuo.

But the first thing that menacing man did was bow to Celty. "You've really saved me this time, Celty."

"Mr. Shiki! You're all right!"

"Yes, somehow. Good job figuring out we were underground."

"We snuck in the rear side, then found a guard and threatened him into telling us where you were," she typed.

"I don't think you *needed* to threaten them," Shiki noted.

"Huh? Actually, now that you mention it, he was, like, laughing and crying at the same time… It was a very strange reaction…"

"I bet. In any case, it's a good thing you showed up here first. I can leave these teenagers with you while the fighting happens," he said, glancing at Kuon and Himeka.

This was enough to tell Yahiro that the man wasn't a threat—but then he had a horrible realization.

"Wait…does that mean this man…*wasn't* one of the kidnappers?" he asked, looking down at the unconscious bald man at his feet.

The man with the piercing gaze just smirked and said, "We were the ones who jumped you with the wrong idea first, so don't worry. He'll be too embarrassed to tell anyone he got knocked out by a high school student, and I'll make sure he doesn't."

Yahiro felt relieved and bowed again. "I see. Please give him my apologies when he comes to."

Ordinarily, he would want to wake the man up and apologize directly, but there was no time for that now. He turned back to his friends.

"Let's get out of here. Things are going to turn dicey."

But Himeka shook her head. "Wait. I can't leave my sister behind."

"Oh, that's right. Your sisters were kidnapped, too. I guess they're not keeping them in here with you," Celty typed, trying to reassure

Himeka. *"I'll be the decoy, so you join the others and escape out the back when you get the chance. All right?"*

"...No. You don't understand, Celty."

"Huh?"

To Celty's surprise, Himeka bit her lip, then explained, "Both of my sisters...are part of the kidnapping group..."

"Wha...? Wh-what does that mean?!" she exclaimed.

Shiki gave her a sardonic answer:

"I'll tell you what it means. This all happened because you spent too much time relaxing on vacation."

♂♀

Mansion area

"...What are you Dragon Zombie scrubs doing around here?"

"You think that doesn't apply to you? If Jan-Jaka-Jan's meeting is up in Hachioji, does that mean you're finally takin' your asses out of Ikebukuro for good?"

Multiple groups were gathering at the mansion lot, which naturally led to some exhibitions of gang rivalry. The senior members of both Dragon Zombie and Jan-Jaka-Jan understood the situation and were taking it in stride, but the hotheaded lower members were starting scuffles here and there.

"Oh yeah? You guys ain't with these fuckin' kidnappers, are you?"

"Quit howlin', Awakusu dogs. Are your noses so bad that you can't tell our scent from these filthy kidnappers?"

"Huhnnn?"

"Uh-huh!"

They started growling and motioning across the way toward each other. A distant camera was recording the entire thing.

"Well, that's just great. The people inside the mansion must have noticed by now."

In a corner of a nearby parking garage, Aoba had a handheld video camera rolling from inside the van.

"Your voice is getting recorded."

"It's fine—I can edit that out later."

"So when are we supposed to go and raid them anyway?" his friend asked.

"Once we know who it is," Aoba answered. "Depending on the answer, it might lead to a fight between Dragon Zombie and Jan-Jaka-Jan, so that might be our cue to move."

Another one of his companions, who was peering through a set of binoculars with night vision, warned them of some action at the scene. "Hey, the group's heading for the mansion entrance."

"Let's see… Uh-oh, that's not Jan-Jaka-Jan. That's one level higher. The scary gentlemen from the Awakusu-kai," Aoba muttered, using the zoom feature of the camera.

There was already a bit of a fight happening near the entrance.

"Oooh, is it starting? How is this one going to play out…?" Aoba wondered aloud, gleefully observing the action. Then he noticed a flickering light in the upper left corner of the screen. "Huh?"

By the time he noticed the small flame, the point of light had already grown in size, describing an arc from the second floor of the mansion toward the outside of the grounds.

A Molotov?!

The moment he recognized it, there was the sound of shattering glass, and flames spread rapidly across the ground.

"Whaaa—?! The hell is this?!"

"Who did that?!"

"Was it *you* assholes?!"

The Molotov cocktail seemed to come from nowhere.

And given the volatile state of the two gangs, it was just the right spark to ignite them.

As soon as the first person threw a punch, a brawl erupted in all places at once.

"Awww, just look at how aggressive these guys are. Jan-Jaka-Jan gets so ornery when they're against us, and the reverse is just as true," said Libei with exasperation. He watched the fight breaking out from a distance. "But now that it's started, there's nothing else to do."

While he sounded regretful, his eyes glittered with pleasure.

A number of younger Jan-Jaka-Jan members rushed up on him from behind with metal pipes.

"Die, Libeiiii!" they screamed, swinging their weapons. Libei spun around, flashing something silver.

The pipes clanged loudly as they struck metal—but then they fell into pieces and clattered on the ground.

Dumbfounded, Jan-Jaka-Jan saw that he was holding in each hand a *liuyedao*, a single-edged saber. After a quick comparison between the sorry state of their pipes and their opponent's curved blades, they shrieked and fled.

"Those must be their newest recruits, then. It's so hard to find good muscle these days." Libei chuckled, shaking his head.

He headed onward, not to stop his companions but to take part in the newly beginning festival and see the conclusion from its midst.

Meanwhile, the younger members of the Awakusu-kai recognized that the projectiles were thrown from inside the mansion. While they were momentarily startled by the attack, they quickly pressed toward the entrance, shouting angrily.

This elicited a new Molotov, aimed right for where they gathered.

And that wasn't all. Flaming bottles flew from other adjacent properties, too, toward any and all groups approaching the mansion. Among the items thrown was something like tear gas. The Shijima Group's property was thrown into instant chaos.

"Shit! Hey, get the guns!"

"No, you idiot! Aozaki will kill us!"

"We can't just sit back and take this!"

"Where's Izumii?! Send him in with a weapon!"

"No way! Fire's the one thing Izumii's afraid of!"

As screams and shouts filled the air, someone even tried to drive their vehicle into the mansion. The sounds of destruction broke the silence of the forest, and the flames from the Molotov cocktails shone against the smoke of the tear gas, lighting up the night.

"This is getting crazy now," murmured Aoba as he caught the event on video.

"Hey, what happened to that Yahiro kid?"

"He's meeting with the Headless Rider. And whenever I show up around her, she makes an unpleasant face...or...unpleasant gesture, I guess."

"So you're just going to ignore them?"

"No, I'm very eager to see how the Headless Rider and Yahiro will react. Capturing that reaction on video is practically why I'm doing this," Aoba said, grinning to himself.

And right on cue with his hopes...

Qrrrrrrrrrrrhhhhhhhh!

An engine roar like the whinnying of a horse cut through the havoc and destruction at the mansion.

The fiercest reaction to that eerie engine sound came from the people inside the building.

"That sound... I know that sound... It's the Headless Rider's motorcycle!"

"You're right! Where...where is it?!"

Aya and Ai, who had been throwing flaming bottles from the upstairs of the mansion, looked about with tears of joy streaming down their cheeks. Aya leaned out the window, searching for the source of the sound.

Then, among the glow of the fire and billowing smoke, atop the roof of the adjacent home, she saw something incredible.

It was the source of their twisted faith—the Headless Rider, Celty Sturluson.

"Oh...ohhh... She's come... She's finally come! She's here to save us!" Aya exclaimed, weeping, as she beheld the sight of Celty atop her motorcycle on the roof.

However, her sister Ai lifted a trembling finger. "Aya... Who is...*that*?"

She was pointing at a shadow of pitch-black, seated right *behind* the rider.

It was darkness *incarnate*.

If the Headless Rider was wearing a riding suit the color of darkness, this was more like the writhing smoke from dry ice condensed into the shape of a human being.

But who was it?

Was it even a person?

The only people to ask these questions were the scant few who actually noticed them on the roof.

But in the next moment, every single person present would become aware of the shadow man.

"_____"

A roar bellowed from the rooftop.

It tore through the night and extinguished all the screams below.

The men punching one another, and even those fleeing from the flames, found themselves pausing in the midst of the action.

The roar sent them a signal that their animal instinct obeyed.

Overwhelming fear drowned out the encroaching flames and the enemy combatants nearby.

"What…is…that?" gasped one of the bikers, but no one could answer that question.

In Ikebukuro, the Headless Rider was a known quantity, a monster everyone knew.

But the monster behind her was a complete unknown.

The hairs on the back of every person's neck rose sharply.

The only sounds left were the hum of the flames and the coughing of those afflicted by tear gas. One of the bikers couldn't hold it in any longer and threw his metal pipe at the figure on the roof.

"Who the hell are you?!" a biker yelled.

The shadow easily grabbed the hurled pipe, however—then started running down the roof. It seemed like he was going to leap right off, but instead he dropped to the veranda on the second floor and faced off against the "kidnappers" there.

On the second floor of the other mansion was a group of about five large, strong men. When they saw the shadow man reaching for them,

trying to destroy their flaming bottles, the men screamed, "Wh-what do you want?" and tried to grab him.

They were easily beaten and subdued.

The Awakusu-kai and the fighting gang members near the entrance to the mansion grounds heard the screams from the second floor and nearly wilted. The men upstairs, despite the dulling sensation of the Heaven's Slave, were experiencing a fear so great that it overpowered the effect of the drug.

"Hey, now! Let's kill 'em!" said the Awakusu-kai's young hotshots, who rushed among the kidnappers and began pounding them into the ground.

"Die, bitch!"

There was no stopping their momentum now. Once their opponents were on the ground, they kicked viciously at their ribs and heads. At the current rate, someone was certain to die—when an upstairs window burst spectacularly as the shadow man leaped through it.

With unnatural speed, he reached the younger yakuza and darted right into their midst.

"Wh-what do you want?! Whose side are you on?!" one of the men snarled, alarmed by the sudden interruption. He tried to punch the shadow.

But the shadow man evaded the punch narrowly, grabbed the wrist, and twisted the attacker's body.

"Guah?!"

"Aaah! Graaah!"

The Awakusu-kai growled and shouted, ganging up on the stranger. He easily shrugged them off and rushed right into the chaos outside.

He took part in whatever fighting he came across, whether Jan-Jaka-Jan or Dragon Zombie, kidnappers or Awakusu-kai.

But he wasn't just throwing punches at random; he went to the most violent fighting around at any one moment and struck at both sides, drawing their hostility toward himself.

Almost as though, by making himself their mutual enemy, he was attempting to neutralize the hostilities happening all around.

Wait, is that…Yahiro? Aoba wondered, staring through the camera's viewfinder.

He had realized that the absolute efficiency of the way the figure was fighting so many at once looked extremely similar to the video of the boy fighting against Shizuo Heiwajima.

"Ah-ha-ha-ha-ha! Did you hear that sound?"

One other man had figured out the identity of the shadow—Libei Ying. He spoke with great entertainment to his sisters, who had approached at some point.

"Listen to the delight in your voice, Yahiro..."

Several minutes later, the shadow man had completed his run through the chaotic battlefield of flame and smoke, then leaped nimbly up the wall of the building and made his way into one of the rooms.

There were two young women there: the sisters of Himeka Tatsugami.

"What...*are* you...? What are you?!"

Aya grappled with subliminal terror at the vision before her.

It wasn't the Headless Rider.

It was some other monster entirely, something they did not know.

"What are you to the Headless Rider...to the Great Celty...?"

To Aya and Ai, who were under the delusion they were becoming part of an urban legend, the existence of this shadow had dumped freezing cold water over their heads.

With his inhuman agility and appearance, he easily crippled their group. It was as though his very presence said, *Normal humans like you are not fit for the Headless Rider.*

"What are youuu?!" Aya screamed and hurled her bottle.

The shadow man grabbed the Molotov cocktail out of the air and used his blackened palm to extinguish the flame on the fuse.

"As you can see...I'm a monster."

♂♀

Ten minutes earlier, basement

"Aaaaargh! Oh no...I'm the caaaause!" Celty typed dramatically. She rolled around on the floor. *"Whaaat. What? Whaaat?! What does this*

mean?! A cult that worships me...? What is that?! I have no idea what that is! I've never even heard of it!"

She was an undignified sight, far short of the glory of the legendary Headless Rider. Himeka and Kuon were dumbstruck, but Yahiro was more familiar with Celty's human side and rubbed her shoulder, asking "Are you all right?"

"Good grief. Every one of them would lose their faith if they saw you now," Shiki muttered.

Celty bolted to her feet. "That's it! If I make an appearance and tell them to knock off all this nonsense, that should solve everything, shouldn't it?!"

"I'm not so sure. If the Heaven's Slave is making them all irrational, they could probably tell themselves they have to destroy the real thing to protect their teachings. But I bet they'll just say, 'The real Headless Rider wouldn't say that,' and treat you like a fake."

"No! Then what should I do?!" Celty panicked.

"The rest is our job," Shiki reassured her. "The suspicions about you have been cleared. While you might have been the start of all of this, the Awakusu-kai isn't going to hold you responsible for any of it. Don't worry."

But Celty only felt more depressed after that answer; she picked up on the implicit threat that she owed him a favor now.

"Wait a minute... What about my sister? Both of my sisters?" asked Himeka.

"...I don't imagine they'll do anything as rash as rounding up a dozen or more civilians to whack 'em...but considering the chaos that's about to break out, I can't guarantee they won't be hurt."

"Oh no..."

Himeka wanted to do something to help. If he kept telling her not to go, she was likely to rush off alone to rescue her sisters.

"What if I just tie everyone up to immobilize them before they start fighting? That way the Awakusu-kai won't do anything drastic, right?"

"...True, that might make it possible to hand over everyone but their ringleader Shijima to the police or hospital," Shiki replied.

But another voice disagreed. "I don't think you should do that..."

"Why not, Kuon?" Celty typed.

Kuon grimaced wryly and said, "Listen...your sisters worship the very idea of Celty...and I know a girl who worships Izaya Orihara in the same way. And if she got treated by Izaya like he didn't need or want her anymore, she'd probably kill herself on the spot."

Why is he bringing up Izaya here?! Celty thought with shock.

But Kuon continued, "If Celty stops all of them directly, at least one or two, if not many more, are going to suffer permanent mental trauma. And your older sister has it especially bad, right?"

"...I won't deny it," Himeka murmured, looking the tiniest bit downcast.

Celty was trying to think of a better idea when Yahiro spoke up and suggested, "Then I'll do it."

"Huh?"

"I'll subdue them all. Um, including Tatsugami's sisters and, depending on the situation, the whatever-kai people."

"What are you talking about, Yahiro? You know you can't..."

But Yahiro just smiled at Celty's attempt to talk sense into him. "Weren't you the one telling me to do this? You said, 'Be a monster.'"

"That's not the same thing..."

But she couldn't stop him. Yahiro was already taking off his jacket and warming up his shoulders.

"What are you saying, Yahiro? Why would you do something so dangerous...?"

"Hey, man, are you serious?"

Yahiro paid heed to Himeka and Kuon, considered their words, and said, "See, I never had any special talents except for violence."

"..."

"I'm not as strong as you two. I spent all my time trying to run away from reality."

It was pure honesty, straight from the heart.

Now that he knew both Himeka's and Kuon's pasts, it occurred to Yahiro that he might not have been able to overcome what they did.

They were strong at heart. But he was weak. All he had was a talent for violence.

"But...how should I say this? If there's an opportunity for me to connect with the rest of the world again, I think it has to be through violence."

"..."

"Yeah, I think I'm just crazy."

He laughed to himself, accepting something he'd resisted. It was the most alive Kuon and Himeka had ever seen Yahiro look.

"So at the very least…I want to live without regrets."

He carefully folded up his jacket and started to tie it around his head.

Celty realized what he was trying to do. *"Oh, you want to hide your face?"*

"I don't want to worry my family or cause any trouble for them… I'm afraid they'll get hurt in some way if people identify me."

"For attempting something so bold, you're cautious in the strangest ways," Celty typed, showing him the screen.

Yahiro gave her a troubled smile and said, "…No, I'm just a coward."

The sight of that smile told Celty that it was pointless to stop him.

She'd seen a number of boys like him in her life. This wasn't the face of a person who would change his mind based on what others thought.

She lifted and dropped her shoulders, mimicking a sigh—then exuded thick, writhing shadow fabric from her palms.

"At the very least, I can give you a mask to hide your identity."

The moment she tried to hand over the mysterious cloth fashioned from shadow, she heard a heavy sigh behind her back.

"So you're just going to move ahead on this without consulting me?"

"Oh…Mr. Shiki, this is, um…for the benefit of the Awakusu-kai, too. I mean, you know, it's not good for you if these amateurs start killing one another, right?" Celty explained in a panicked rush.

Shiki ignored her, stood before Yahiro, and assessed him.

"Hey, boy."

"…Yes?"

"You said you'd deal with everyone, including 'the whatever-kai people.' Do you understand what you're saying there?"

"…"

Yahiro was silent, so Shiki continued, "Aren't you going to consider what might happen if they decide to go after your family as retribution?"

"If it happens," Yahiro said, pausing momentarily. Then he concluded, "I'll just have to finish the job…"

It wasn't sarcasm or a joke. It was just a truthful answer.

Shiki met his clear, straightforward gaze with narrowed eyes.

Then he smirked and said to Celty, "You're right, then. He *is* a monster."

"...*What?*"

"Well, I guess nobody can stop a mysterious, unidentified monster from doing its thing," Shiki said, implicitly approving the boy's plan. But he wasn't done. "However, if 'the whatever-kai people' suffer any deaths or lifelong injuries as a result..."

His voice was endlessly cold and unfathomably sharp.

"If that happens...I'm going to skin your monster's hide for a trophy, boy."

♂♀

Present moment, mansion roof

Shiki's words echoed in Yahiro's mind.

Ultimately, though, it was the look in his eyes that was the greatest source of fear to Yahiro that day—and the last.

It's strange.

With this shadow wrapped around me...so many things just don't scare me anymore.

When he accepted that he was willing to become a monster and wore the shadow Celty gave to him, the fear within Yahiro simply vanished.

That was vital for him.

It was the fear that always drove him to overdo his reactions to every opponent. But with the fear weakened, he was no longer desperate, and now he could hold back his strength, staying short of his maximum.

Either wearing Celty's shadow or taking her words to heart—or both—had an effect on him. He didn't know the exact reason why, but now, in this moment that he was acting as a true, complete monster, Yahiro was freed from his fear.

He subdued Himeka's sisters, not hard enough to hurt them, and he tied them up with the bedsheet he found in the room before climbing back up to the roof.

He was filled with great satisfaction, though it was a different kind than what he felt when fighting Shizuo Heiwajima with all his strength.

It was probably just an illusion.

Whether it was for the sake of another or not, violence was violence.

He was using Himeka as an excuse to punch other people.

Yahiro knew these things—but he was still happy.

He was happy being evil, or a monster, or a hypocrite.

The point was that, by becoming a monster of his own volition, he had taken a step outside of the world he'd been trapped inside his whole life.

For the first time ever, he felt something like acceptance—and once again, he lifted his face to the sky and roared.

"Wow. Amazing! Amazing, amazing, amazing! I can't believe I just got to see a superhero in action!"

The bikers had lost all will to fight after the sudden, overwhelming appearance of the monster—except for Libei Ying, who was in a celebratory mood.

"Or is he more of a villain or fiend? Either one is fine. The point is, he's cool."

Libei put his *liuyedao* away over his back and clapped and cheered like a child.

"I want you on my team even more than before, Yahiro Mizuchi," he said, suddenly serious. "Or…perhaps I should call you a nameless monster. One that shouldn't exist…"

Then he turned to his sisters with a smile, like he'd just come up with a great idea.

"Hey, what do you think? Should we call that monster…Snake Hands?"

"Oh, it's really getting good now…"

Aoba turned off the camera. A smile of pure glee tugged at his lips.

"That monster—well, it's just Yahiro—has now made an enemy out of every group in the city and also made allies out of every group in the city."

"What does that mean?"

"It means that since the Dollars ended, there's finally a new festival in town. Before, a gang made the city dance. This time, it's the opposite."

Despite his boyish looks, Aoba Kuronuma wore an expression of great evil. He smirked at the monster on the roof and muttered to himself, "Now...how will you use your power to change Ikebukuro...?"

Thus, on this night, the birthing cry of a new monster, raucous and raw, graced the streets of Tokyo.

That sound, caught on film by Aoba, would spread like wildfire on the Internet—and, in the span of less than a day, would become the source of a new urban legend.

As though the city itself were touting the existence of its newest monster.

EPILOGUE

EPILOGUE A
The Founder

On the Ikebukuro information site IkeNew! Version I.KEBU.KUR.O

Popular Post: [Birth of an Urban Legend] Does the Headless Rider have a boyfriend?!

"A new urban legend escorted by the Headless Rider" (Rehosted from *Tokyo Warrior* online site)

In the middle of April, eyewitness reports started coming in, saying the famous urban legend, the Headless Rider, had returned to Ikebukuro.

But did you know that a new urban legend became the hot new topic around the same time?

Footage uploaded to an online video site shows what appears to be a battle between rival motorcycle gangs late at night. The sudden appearance of the Headless Rider in their midst seems to bring the battle under control—but the problem is that the figure who used force to bring an end to the fighting was not actually the Headless Rider.

A silent motorcycle that transforms into a headless horse. A headless rider who swings a pitch-black scythe. And what he or she brought along: another mysterious being.

It was covered in flickering black shadow all over—even its face.

And with incredible strength and agility, it defeated the brawling combatants one after the other.

All alone, this new being took on dozens and overwhelmed them single-handedly.

So who is this new urban legend?

The Ikebukuro-centric writer Shinichi Tsukumoya said this in an entry on his blog: "Tired of giving birth to legends, the Headless Rider has brought back an heir. Perhaps the six-month disappearance was actually just a trip in search of the next urban legend."

—(The rest of this article can be read at the original link)

Comment from IkeNew! *Administrator*

A new boyfriend, the Headless Rider has.

I have often claimed that the Headless Rider was a woman, but now it turns out a real player, she is.

The Black Rider and Black Warrior. A very good combination, it is. Always together, wherever they go, inseparable.

Around the folks in Dragon Zombie, it seems the new monster has acquired the name of Snake Hands.

Therefore, for the sake of convenience, on this site, the abbreviation *SH* to the new monster, we shall refer.

Widen even further, the world does. May the day soon come that it appears in the dictionary.

Apparently, the missing green-haired boy was rescued by these two, and found safe, he was.

The Headless Rider has a boyfriend, and a happy ending is enjoyed by all.

Happily ever after. Ever after?

Admin: Rira Tailtooth Zaiya

♂♀

Shinra's apartment

"Happily *never* after!" exclaimed Shinra, after reading the news article. He rolled back atop the sofa. "Happily not at all! I am not happy in the least about this, Celty. Cellltyyy!"

"Why, what's wrong? Do you have brain worms?"

"Just look at this article! They're spreading terrible false stories about you having a boyfriend, and it's not even about me!"

"What if they're not false stories?" she teased.

Shinra's face went pale. He shouted, "If...if that happens, I won't give you away! I'll fight that Yahiro boy!"

He brandished his fists, ready for battle; Celty had told him all about what happened at the mansion.

"You know he's a match for Shizuo."

"...I'll challenge him to a contest of medical vocabulary terms!"

"Don't be childish!" she snapped.

But Shinra kept rolling. "Waaah! Everything about this makes me angry! They claim they worship you, Celty, but they don't build a single statue of you?! I would have taken a 3D scan of you while you were sleeping and mass-produced life-size Celtys ages ago!"

"I'm sorry, can we rewind and discuss that for just a second?!"

Later, once she had calmed Shinra down a bit, Celty thought back on her time with Yahiro.

"I wonder who it was that taught him there was a monster in Ikebukuro."

"Hmm?" Shinra wondered.

She decided to touch on the boy's past for context. *"Well, Yahiro said he came to Tokyo because he was fighting in his hometown once and a tourist told him there was an even more incredible monster in Ikebukuro."*

"...Hmmmm?" Shinra murmured again. He considered this for a moment. "Where did you say this Yahiro boy came from?"

"He said he was from Akita."

Then Shinra smacked a fist into his palm. He had the answer.

"Oh. That was *me*."

*   *   *

"*...Huh?*"

"Remember the day after the Omagari Fireworks Festival, when we stopped by that hot spring in Haburagi?"

"*Oh, right...that out-of-the-way spot.*"

"I was going for a little walk there when I happened to spot a boy who'd gotten all bloody in a fight. I remember talking to him about something like that."

Wow, what a funny coincidence—they laughed...and then Celty set the font size to maximum and shoved her phone in Shinra's face.

"*You...you were the one who dragged him into this!*"

"Um, I suppose I was."

"*I don't believe it... When the article said the Headless Rider was going on a pilgrimage across the country and scouting out an heir, it was more or less accurate!*"

"...Oh noooo! What have I done?!"

Shinra looked absolutely distraught.

"Have I summoned my own romantic rival here to Ikebukuro?! Have I given myself a valentine's present of trials and tribulations?! Give mercy to your enemies, they say...but I've given a stranger mercy, and his character class upgraded into 'romantic rival'! I'm screwed... That's it, Celty—I'll become a monster, too! So spin off a little of that shadow you're wearing and share it with me, or alternatively you can wrap us both up toge*ther—blfhg!*"

"*Stop trying to grope me in the middle of the conversation!*"

Celty pushed him off her, feeling keenly aware that their normal life had returned. Now that the missing people had reappeared, the ugly kidnapping rumors were dying out, and it felt like far fewer people were calling Celty a kidnapper anymore.

Savoring the feeling of normalcy for himself as well, Shinra said, "By the way...whatever happened with the Tatsugami family?"

"*Oh...safely hospitalized, I heard. That Shijima guy was forcing them to take the drug, but neither Mr. Shiki nor Kuon have submitted a criminal complaint, so it's not clear if he'll be charged with anything or not.*"

She continued:

"*The rest is an issue for the family to sort out, I suppose.*"

♂♀

Raira General Hospital, private room

Though the effects of the drug were still racking their bodies, it was the fifth day after the incident when the "true believers" of Celty finally began to regain a measure of sanity.

"They said Ai will be able to leave soon," Himeka told her older sister.

Aya rolled over onto her side to look at her and said quietly, "...You were the one who was right in the end."

"That's not true. You just went about it the wrong way. It's very touching that you were thinking of everyone's happiness," Himeka said.

Aya smiled sadly. "You...really are strong."

"You think too highly of me."

"And that's why the Headless Rider chose you instead of me..."

"That has nothing to do with it. I can introduce you sometime."

Even that casual mention of being a go-between brought a pained smile to Aya's face. "I don't deserve to meet her. She could kill me for what I did to her, and I'd deserve it."

"No...she's not like that." Himeka sighed.

Aya went ahead and asked something that had been weighing on her mind. "So...why did the Gre...the Headless Rider disappear for half a year?"

It was an act that led to their despair, so despite knowing that any blame would be misplaced, she couldn't help but wonder.

Himeka thought for a moment, then revealed the truth as it had been told to her. "On a hot springs vacation."

"..."

"..."

Time between the two came to a stop.

Eventually, Aya broke the silence with a tremulous "Hot springs... vacation...?"

"Yes... All over the place... Akita, Kyushu...," Himeka said, nodding.

Aya was dumbfounded. Then, like a dam bursting, she laughed.

"Ha...ah-ha-ha-ha...ha-ha-ha-ha... What does that mean? A hot springs vacation..."

She laughed and laughed for an entire minute, until her voice was muffled with tears.

"She went off visiting hot springs for half a year...without a care in the world...and that's who I was dedicating my entire life to?"

She laughed and cried at the joke her life had become, and Himeka just watched.

"You were right, Himeka. Maybe...this really is just how the world works," Aya said and apologized sadly. Himeka just shook her head with that flat, expressionless look on her face.

"I'm not saying I accept it for what it is."

"Huh...?"

"But I can't bring myself to hate this life. I have Dad, Mom, you, Ai...all the family I love. So I decided that I didn't want to run... I wanted to bring everyone happiness."

She took her older sister's hand, determined to say the thing she hadn't been able to say before.

"The world might not be fair, but that doesn't mean it can't be changed."

"You still think of me...as family...?" Aya asked, unsure. Himeka was puzzled as to why she would doubt such an obvious thing.

Aya turned away from her sister and looked out the window. The tears streaming from her eyes were for a different reason now.

"You really are strong, Himeka."

When Himeka exited the hospital, Yahiro was waiting for her.

"How is she?"

"She's doing much better now," Himeka replied.

He looked as relieved as though he were hearing about his own family. "That's good. So you can go back to the way your family used to be."

"...Yes. Although I'm not sure if I'd say it's the way it 'used to be'..."

"What do you mean?" he asked, without a moment's hesitation. But Himeka didn't seem bothered by that.

She explained the particular circumstances of her home life. Yahiro listened to her describe the problems with her mother. It seemed to put an idea in his head.

"I'm betting that your mom left herself on the far side of that shadow on the wall."

"Huh?"

"The part of herself she doesn't like… The weak part of herself that might take out her pain on her daughters," Yahiro said, choosing his words carefully. "You know how in that fairy tale, the barber who sees that the king has donkey ears goes and shouts it into the hole in the tree? I think she's taking the part of her she wants to hide, the part that she might turn into one day, and locking it behind the shadow on the wall."

"Why do you think that?" Himeka inquired, wary that he might be saying that just to make her feel better.

She was not expecting the answer he gave her.

"Because that's how it was for me."

"…For you?"

"I was a huge coward, and I was terrified of the people who came to hurt me. Deep down, in the most honest part of my heart, I thought that the quickest solution was to kill them before they killed me. Only then could I rest easy."

"…"

"So in my mind, I kept beating them until they stopped moving. Every single night, I fled into that imaginary world. That way, I could get it out of my system and not do it in reality."

"That never backfired on you?" she asked, an honest question.

Yahiro shrugged. "Maybe it had the opposite effect. But I never actually killed anyone… Then again, I went overboard several times, so I guess it didn't really help in the end…"

He decided that thinking about it wasn't going to bring him the answer, so he just exhaled and grimaced at Himeka.

"I don't know what the right answer is. I'll just have to figure it out as I go."

He looked down at his scarred hands and clenched them.

"That's why I want to be your hands. If you or Kuon or anyone has trouble, I want to use my fists to protect you."

"…I can't believe you said that without feeling embarrassed."

"Really? Am I just weird?"

"Yes. Very," she said bluntly. Then she let her emotions reshape the expression on her face.

It was an emotion that she didn't need to suppress or hide, unlike sadness or anger.

"But I think that's wonderful."

When he saw the gentle smile on her face, Yahiro smiled back, feeling just a little bit bashful.

♂♀

From a distance, Kuon Kotonami watched them go before speaking into his phone.

"Well, darn. You just had to go and spill my secrets. Now they know I've been playing coy this whole time."

"I'm just saying, it's hard for you to act coy with your hair and face done up like that." Nozomi laughed on the other end. *"Anyway, I'll admit, that Yahiro boy is funny. He's too nice for his own good. Even after learning what you're really like, he was constantly worried about you."*

"And what did you say to that, Sis?" he asked, sulking.

Nozomi chirped, *"I told him, 'You don't need to feel responsible for any of this, Yahiro. He only thinks of you as a pawn meant to be used.'"*

"Gee, thanks a lot."

"And what do you think he said to that?"

"?" Kuon couldn't begin to guess.

Nozomi quoted, *"'It doesn't matter.'"*

"It…doesn't matter?"

"No matter the reason, you were the first kids who ever treated him like a normal person. Even after you saw him fighting, you talked to him like normal and didn't freak out about it. He said that really made him happy."

"…"

"And therefore, it was worth risking his life to protect you two. Can you believe that? Just for talking to him like a normal person."

Kuon considered this for a while, then asked, "Did he *really* say that?"

"*Good question. It's up to you whether you believe me or not. You know I make a living on lies and fiction, right?*"

Oh. *He really did say that,* Kuon's instincts told him. He exhaled a long, long breath.

"It doesn't matter what kind of mistaken ideas he's got in his head," he said icily, "I'm just using him for my own ends."

"*Awww. Poor Yahiro.*"

"He's so simpleminded for a guy with such incredible strength," Kuon said with a shrug. He could feel the bile rising.

"That's why I hate humanity."

♂♀

Kotonami home

Once the call was over, Nozomi grinned mischievously at her phone.

"You'll never be a replacement for Izaya."

She was gleeful, delighted, and hiding her true feelings behind that smile.

"Compared to Izaya…you're a teensy bit too nice!"

♂♀

Shinra's apartment

"*I'll admit, Yahiro's a pretty funny guy.*"

"I'm funny, too! Wait, hang on… Let me come up with something funny to say!"

"*Don't hurt yourself,*" Celty typed, comforting her red-faced partner.

In the end, she'd handed over the shadow-crafted mask and body wrap to the boy. She'd already created it for him, after all, and it seemed better to just leave it with him rather than to get rid of it right away.

She'd told him, "*I've never experimented to see how many days it will last on its own, so if it dissipates, just get in touch. When I made a helmet out of it before, there weren't any problems, so it's gentle on skin and hair...I think."*

Yahiro had looked at her, dead serious, and asked, *"Is it safe to wash this?"*

Shinra noticed that she was chuckling to herself. "Hey! Are you laughing as you remember that Yahiro boy, Celty?!"

"You're extremely keen in the strangest ways."

"Wait...something funny...something funny... C-can I tell you a funny story, Celty?!" he begged, practically crying.

Annoyed, Celty typed, *"You're so desperate... Anyway, I should be off duty for a little while again. I suppose listening to you practice your storytelling isn't the worst thing I could be doing."*

"Really?! Wait, so you're not doing courier work for a while?"

"Mr. Shiki asked me to lie low for now. Apparently, there are still people out there who suspect me. But don't worry—I'll look for some other kind of job."

"It's fine, Celty. I'll support you for life! And I'll also be your house-husband, so you can just slob out and do nothing in my presence all day long!" Shinra said, his eyes sparkling.

Exasperated, Celty thrust her smartphone in his face. Her typed message read, *"I don't want a life with nothing to do, either."*

At this point, they weren't aware that in a corner of *IkeNew!*, mixed in among the usual ads, there was one rather strange banner.

It was a small image right at the bottom of the page with the letters *SH* written on it.

Any sharp-eyed visitor who clicked on the image would be taken to a different site with a short message.

We'll solve your Ikebukuro problems.
   Missing persons, revenge against bullies, personal protection:
   We do everything!
      Ikebukuro Mutual Aid Group, Snake Hands

This odd little advertisement would go on to create, contrary to Celty's concerns, a "life with plenty to do."

But she had no idea about that yet.

EPILOGUE B
Or the Next Prologue: The Avenger

"Did you catch Shijima's trail?" Shiki asked his subordinate.

Five days had passed since the end of the incident. But just like on the previous days, the answer to that question was not a positive one.

"No, nothing..."

The Awakusu-kai had confirmed that Shijima was the one who set up the Church of the Headless Rider. They'd learned as much from the testimony of the true believers who had been hospitalized and had come back to their senses.

"And it doesn't sound like he sensed us coming and ran off, either."

Not everyone they found at that mansion was deeply devoted to the Headless Rider, taking drugs to escape reality. Some of them were Shijima's old friends, lured with money and drugs to serve as temporary bodyguards. The basement guard who Shiki had attacked was one of them.

But none of those people knew where Shijima had gone.

So it was true that Shijima started the group, but it seemed the believers had taken over and built it up from there. After a while, he no longer had any contact with them. The only thing that passed from him to them was money and Heaven's Slave.

The Awakusu-kai tried to threaten his grandfather, the head of the Shijima Group, and his executive father, but they said their son had been missing for over a year.

What could that petty criminal be plotting now? It was slightly eerie.

"Good grief… I thought I'd have less to worry about with that info broker out of the picture," Shiki muttered as he stared out the window of the agency.

"I suppose it's just the nature of this job that every time one problem disappears, another appears to take its place…"

♂♀

Tokyo—office interior

A small rental office was located inside a larger office building.

On the floor above was a group conducting phone scams. Anyone listening could hear all kinds of strange conversations coming through the ceiling.

In this space, however, there was just a single chair upon which a man sat.

Bandages were wrapped around the upper half of his head, leaving only a small crack through which his eyes stared at nothing in particular.

A woman's willowy hand clung to his shoulders. There were many, many scars on her fingers, which traced his neck seductively.

"So Izaya Orihara…did not involve himself in this case," she said.

"That's true."

"What do you think? Is he really dead?"

"I don't care either way. As long as I can avenge myself, that's all that matters. Izaya Orihara is secondary."

The woman seemed surprised by this. "Oh…? I thought that you were looking for revenge *against* Izaya Orihara. I guess I was wrong."

"What about you, Earthworm?" asked Shijima, his voice cold.

The woman he called Earthworm put a finger to her lips and hummed. "Hmm… I don't know. But I did hate him, so I suppose if I have the chance to kill him, I'll consider myself lucky."

She giggled to herself, but it was difficult to tell whether she was actually joking about that.

She laid her cheek against Shijima's head and asked, "If you don't care about Izaya Orihara, who do you want revenge against? The Headless Rider? Shizuo Heiwajima? Akabayashi from the Awakusu-kai?"

Shijima's voice was flat. "The city."

There was a quiet madness in his eyes. Anyone who knew him in years past would have asked the same question: *Is this really Shijima?*

The changed man fixed his gaze on empty space, envisioning the sight beyond it, declaring his intentions.

"I've decided to get revenge on the city of Ikebukuro."

"Well, that's quite the task. And what do you plan to do?"

"Nothing."

There was no emotion on Shijima's face. He merely spoke into nothingness, paying no attention to Earthworm and her voluptuous body.

"The seeds of atrocity litter the ground throughout the city. But most of them die out before they ever sprout."

"I'm simply going to give them a little bit of water…and fertilizer to help them grow."

As he said, even now, after the winds of the Dollars and Izaya Orihara had passed, the seeds brought in had remained in the city.

Would they bloom into good or evil?

No one could say the answer at this point.

And thus, with the madness of this disgruntled avenger contained within it, the city began to weave a new story.

As it ever would, so long as people existed there.

TO BE CONTINUED DURARARA!!SH×3
©2014 Ryohgo Narita

CAST

Yahiro Mizuchi
Kuon Kotonami
Himeka Tatsugami

Aoba Kuronuma

Kururi Orihara
Mairu Orihara

Akane Awakusu

Nozomi Kotonami

Aya Tatsugami
Ai Tatsugami

Libei Ying

Shiki

Shizuo Heiwajima

Celty Sturluson
Shinra Kishitani

AFTERWORD

What's coming in the next volume?

The Kotonami siblings have started a rather fishy-sounding business, and they've hired Celty for something, even dragging Yahiro and Himeka into it, too! On top of that, who is this mysterious pair who comes to call on their services, and why do they only speak in references to anime and manga…?

Hi again. It's me, Narita.

Who are they, you ask? They're obviously Yumasaki and Karisawa from the original series. But they aren't the only ones who will show up. There will be lots of characters, like always, so if you're not a fan of Yumasaki and Karisawa, look forward to the others!

…And now we can set aside the matter of the next volume…

By the way, have you ever taken a close look at the spines of the volumes in the original Japanese release from Dengeki Bunko?

If you were to consult the spine for the Japanese edition of this book, for example, there is a code that reads "NA-9-50." That means that this book is by the ninth author whose name starts with *Na* who has debuted under Dengeki Bunko, and it is that author's fiftieth book overall.

Yes, my fiftieth book.

It's been ten years since I debuted with Dengeki Bunko. This is the fiftieth book I have published through Dengeki Bunko under the name Ryohgo Narita!

When I started, I had no idea if I would even get a second book, but I've been very fortunate to continue. Somehow I've reached a grand total of fifty. This is all thanks to everyone at the editorial office who has helped me, and even more than that, all you readers who have supported me. Thank you so much!

I'm going to take care of myself and continue on my way to the next big milestone!

Now, as for my auspicious fiftieth published book, *Durarara!! SH*, Vol. 2, this marks the end of the first story arc. Some of the characters who were only briefly introduced, like Libei Ying, should become major players in the next book. Look forward to it!

Now that the Kotonami siblings and Celty are going to embark on some fishy business, my intention is to do stand-alone stories starting with the third volume. I don't have any plans for lengthy five-volume story arcs like the ones around Mikado in the original *Durarara!!* series...for now. I'm keeping my options open.

As for the *Durarara!!* anime, there were lots of announcements at the Dengeki Bunko Fall Festival 2014 event just before this book came out.

The cast is fantastic. Not only the actors from the first season returning to their roles, but also the incredible new people we have stepping in to fill the new roles. I've been flabbergasted ever since I heard the news.

I can't wait to see how they handle the original *Durarara!!* series up through Volume 13. I'm going to do my best with this new series to keep the train rolling!

If possible, I'm hoping to put out some other books in the meantime...but the problem is, I have a lot of intensive work squashed into my schedule, which makes it hard to find time for new books... But I can say that my collaboration with TYPE-MOON titled *Fate/strange Fake* is still ongoing. As long as I don't get sick, I should be delivering one of those this winter.

You can always check out the precise street dates in *Dengeki Bunko Magazine*, the Dengeki Bunko website and e-mail list, and my Twitter account. If you happen to see any of those, check up on those dates!

And the anime isn't the only cross-media adaptation in the works.

There are preparations underway for a new video game, and multiple serialized manga are currently ongoing!

Speaking of manga, I can only write words and am unable to draw storyboards at all. In the last ten years, though, I've been blessed to see many artists turn my writing into manga, as well as animators put my stories into motion. I'm full of admiration for the way that artists can create a sense of space of their own. I hope I can improve my own writing to be able to create that same sense of image and motion inside your head as you read...

These adaptations have always had the benefit of expanding the world of my stories, so if I'm fortunate, that relationship will continue.

I pray that there will be many more experiences (hopefully good ones) in the next ten years, as I roll onward toward a hundred volumes. Nothing would make me happier than for you to come along on the journey.

Lastly, my acknowledgments.

To my editor, Papio, and everyone at ASCII Media Works and the printers, I'm sorry for submitting this manuscript even later than last time...

To the excellent folks who are bringing *Durarara!!* to life in different forms of media, between our new anime project, three different manga series, and even a new game.

To the family, friends, authors, and illustrators who support me.

To Suzuhito Yasuda, who squeezed the time out of his busy schedule to do such wonderful pieces of artwork. Congratulations on finishing the *Durarara!!* collaboration manga packed in with each disc release of the *Yozakura Quartet* anime! I loved every last one of them!

But most of all, to you all for picking up the continuation of *Durarara!! SH*.

Thank you, thank you all! I hope that we meet again soon!

• September 2014—Ryohgo Narita